SUBTRACTION

Mary Robison

SUBTRACTION

Alfred A. Knopf   New York

1991

THIS IS A BORZOI BOOK
PUBLISHED BY ALFRED A. KNOPF, INC.

Copyright © 1991 by Mary Robison
All rights reserved under International and Pan-American
Copyright Conventions. Published in the
United States by Alfred A. Knopf, Inc., New York,
and simultaneously in Canada by Random House of
Canada Limited, Toronto. Distributed by
Random House, Inc., New York.

Library of Congress Cataloging-in-Publication Data
Robison, Mary.
Subtraction / Mary Robison. — 1st ed.
p.   cm.
ISBN 0-394-53943-5
I. Title.
PS3568.O317S8
813'.54—dc20   90-53102   CIP

Manufactured in the United States of America
First Edition

for Bobbie Bristol
and, with love,
for Rachel and Jen

SUBTRACTION

COCO PLUMOSO

OH SURE, they, over there in the city, had rain to behold. From out my third-story window I could see to Boston and over to the Fenway. There the sky was so low and black; if I had been *there* the rain would have torn at my hair, and ruffled my clothes, soaked me in cool lashings of rain. But over where I was, not so far west—a six-minute trolley ride!—nothing but fringe winds and hot breezes that dog-bone July day, although the four floor fans I had running were mixing up a nice brisk area on my damp back, which was wet from the ice-water shower I'd just suffered. I made myself do that every hour to cool off: five minutes of a paralyzing cold shower, but then *fifty*-five minutes of relief; of shivering even at first.

A telephone bill that arrived early in July showed Raf's tracks. It showed all the long-distance calls he had charged to our Brookline number. He'd been to D.C.; gone on to Charlottesville; then Birmingham; Oxford, Mississippi;

Thibodaux, Louisiana. New Orleans was last listed, and from there Raf made three Houston calls.

Now I had a chair in the only corner of the room not scorching with light, and I sat, wearing a towel sarong, hair streaming from my hourly shower, and dialed, and watched starlings out the window, and waited for someone in Houston to answer his phone.

The man who said hello was named Raymond Hollander.

He said, "Raf's here in town, I believe, but not *here* here. Not with me, or with us, anymore. And where he'll be tomorrow I wouldn't know. Or, hell, where he'll be tonight. I could make some guesses about him but nothing you'd wanna put a peso down on."

I called Herb, a former student of mine.

"I'll go 'on line,' " Herb said. And, "Hold."

His voice returned. "Window seat; flight's this evening; they can do vegetarian; a motel suite; a week's worth of rental car, but *car* isn't accurate. I splurged on that part."

"You should market these skills, Herb," I said. "You go public, you could buy food."

"They're not skills, they're crimes. And not winky-dink ones either. They're felonies. So think prison, hard time, the gulag . . ."

Herb went on like that. I hung up and dialed again for Raymond Hollander.

Raymond said we could meet tomorrow, after he got off work, at something he called an ice house.

"*Cab* there," he said. " 'Cause directions is tricky and this is in a dumb place, nowhere you wanna be circlin' lost. We'll hook up there, then we'll see."

I studied the road atlas and its blowup of Houston, picturing horses, cacti, oil derricks, astronauts.

Once earlier after Raf vanished for a week, he mentioned an artist had put him up. I realized Raf was talking about my dad.

"You mean *Mario*?"

"In fact," Raf said.

"You stayed with my dad and didn't say anything?"

Raf shrugged his bony shoulders. His face had a stillness that seemed almost shy. I figured that over the years I'd heard plenty of stories, without his being named, of Raymond Hollander.

Houston wasn't desert and cacti. Houston was magnolia and swamp, jungle heat and jungle humid, and Raymond's ice house was in a neighborhood of shotgun shacks.

I had left my rental car—a low, quick, red Firecat—at my hotel and cabbed here.

The place, called the Cielito Lindo, was a stucco garage converted to an outdoor bar.

There was a slab of patio in front where people ordered drinks from a counter, as from a Yankee Dairy Queen, and then the idea was to stand around in the green shade of the corrugated fiberglass roof's overhang.

This was Raf's type of territory—of the spirit and mind—and I was heartened on first view. But the heat ticked like a windup clock; dangerous heat. The patio section emptied.

I moved inside and sat in the attached lounge. It was a wine-smelling cinderblock box with plywood boards banged over its windows. My glasses kept fogging and the frames slid down my wet nose.

I was sinking from the six-hour plane ride, the heat, my second Chihuahua beer.

I thought about the Gauguin show—240 pieces on exhibit at the National in Washington. I could've flown there instead, could've been standing in a cool quiet gallery wing right now, studying "Yellow Christ."

I was afraid Raymond Hollander was like Raf; that he would *mean* to show, but . . .

Mexican music blew from a radio: fast roiling music so that when I closed my eyes I saw dizzying orange skirts swirling off brown legs. When I opened my eyes I saw boxing posters and tangled strings of Christmas bulbs. I saw I was the only woman left in the dark bar and that there were ten or twelve men. None was talking. All were pounding away at drink.

The door made its noise and shapes of light crossed the near wall. Somebody said, "Ray."

He was early-forties, tanned, dressed in rough clothes, their colors worked and washed out by salt, soap, sun bleach. He looked like a desert item, part mirage through my fogged lenses. He looked exactly the sort who might run with Raf.

He came straight over and climbed into the booth seat opposite. He planted a hand on the table deck for a hello.

"Thanks for coming," I said. "He's not out in your car is he?"

Raymond said no, four times, four ways. He called me Mrs. Deveaux.

"I'm just Paige."

"Well, you're not just anything," he said and smiled. His smile was good—white, genuine, a smile you had to repay with one of your own.

I did, but switched instantly to staring at the tabletop.

Its wood looked oily and warm and handled: oily from a century's worth of touch in this cantina.

Raymond said, "It's going to be a leetle trickier than what you mighta thought."

Nodding, I must've appeared so heartsick and tired that Raymond did another smile.

I took off the glasses. I said, "You're either the guy who worked with Raf in Baltimore, or you were on the tramp steamer, or you could be the one with the smart dog. . . . I'm sorry, I get his friends confused."

"So does he," Raymond said. "I'm smart dog—that one."

He shook a pack of Camels. "He was with me for almost three weeks."

"Prevailing on your good will," I said, and Raymond pointed a cigarette in my direction. "No thank you. I meant Raf."

"Now that boy *rilly* prevailed," Raymond said.

I asked, "Could you quit smiling so much?"

Looking me over, he said, "Umm," as if he'd got my height, weight, and bra size.

"You're as tall as I thought you'd be. I never saw Raf with a woman wasn't one of your stretch jobs."

"Stretch jobs," I said, and there was a cry, as if on my behalf, from the street. I couldn't tell if the shriek was made by a kid or a drunk or from joy or terror.

"I'm not saying like rubber band," Raymond said. Above him on the white plaster wall, hand-painted purple roses cavorted. They seemed friends, these flowers, as in a cartoon.

"How many women have you seen Raf *with*?" I asked.

"Umm. However many there are. You're the only one I know of he's married. How long's that been?"

"Five and something years," I said. "So. He crashed your

car, drank your liquor, ate your food." Raymond was nodding yes, yes. "Jumped your wife? Borrowed money?
Cooked your parakeet?"

"Some of those. Yep. Yes, ma'am."

The Cielito Lindo's matchpack was soggy from the tabletop or from just the day, but Raymond got his cigarette
lighted and sighed smoke and appeared to relax. He ordered another Chihuahua for me, an iced tea for himself.
He ordered by yelling at the boy behind the bar.

"I'm sorry for all he did, Raymond. I wish you had him
tied up out in your car, or someplace under guard. I need
to find him, fast like."

Raymond winced and drove a hand through his hair,
which was actually golden, thatchy and thick.

"There are several likely places to look for Raf, though
if he's not in *them*, any of 'em, you're fucked."

"Because that means he's left town?"

"Yeah, and 'cause, you know, he's not too good on
forwarding addresses."

I would say to myself that Raf kept me strung so tight I
sometimes believed I felt the earth turning under my shoe
soles. This is no gift that he brings, I would say, and remember how he came at me in bed—with such heat—as
if each chance were our last on the very last night of the
world. Every time with Raf, I would think—before he
chased the thought away—"This is so scary!"

He had begun to disappear that spring just as the landscape was softening after the violence of Boston winter;
just as green and gold and a little warmth were coming
through the window screens. He'd be gone a week, ten
days. Then he'd be back, and he'd have new scars, new
stories, no excuses.

As Raymond got his car together, the Cielito's glimmering side wall kept me upright. I was dropping, though. I felt brain-cooked.

My thoughts landed on: "This is just a place."

The year before I had spent summer break in Cameroon. My dad, Mario, took me. He was a sculptor and he wanted to see Bamileke and Zambeze art and what architecture remained. Cameroon was hotter than Houston, and wetter, but I came to regard it as just a place. Houston was just a place.

Raymond pulled up now in his convertible, a broad old top down, the clear-green color of a frog pond. All over the sides were furry spray-painted scribbles and scrawls: "JURA!" and "LOS NINOS," and twice in script, "LUISA."

"It's a beaner-mobile," Raymond said. "I use it to drive to work. Nobody's gonna steal it. I work construction. Doors are broke so when I say 'Hop in . . .' "

Riding along, head lolling back, my eyes caught the rim of the sun there, visibly beaming red hydrogen light.

We drove up Bienvenida Boulevard. There were pudgy short palm trees with fronds bowing from their tops.

We passed a baked-clay building marked EL ESTUDIO ESCUELOS CANTOS; next a fence of three hundred hubcaps; now Southwest Texas College's Beam Particles Laboratory, all buff and square.

Ahead, huge cloud forms were piled up and the sky shone the same bluejay blue as the Houston squad car riding with us, driver's side.

"I really appreciate this!" I shouted at Raymond.

He glanced at me, jimmied the gear stick to neutral. We

idled at a railroad crossing while a Union Pacific switcher shunted some fifty tanker cars past.

"It's fun, riding in a convertible," I said.

"This day should be over, though," Raymond said.

My head bobbed yes, but I was a little hurt he thought that.

Whither are we moving? Away from all suns? Are we not plunging continually? Backward, sideward, forward, in all directions? Is there still any up or down? Are we not straying as through an infinite nothing? Do we not feel the breath of empty space? Has it not become colder? Is not night continually closing in on us?

That was Nietzsche, quoted in a kind of goodbye note that Raf left.

"I thought of a place," Raymond said. "We'll be lucky or we won't."

We jounced over the train tracks after the guard gate's arm lifted. We passed a Fiesta, a food market with brass noise coming from loudspeakers over its entry doors. We went by scrap-metal yards, and a building titled O.K. CREDIT USED CARS AND TRUCKS.

Raymond's engine was missing bad. He fought the stick for each gear shift. His suspension was blown.

We banged along beside a broad cement ditch—Buffalo Bayou.

"All right, darlin'," he said. "This is gonna be rancid."

"I'm ready."

He looked over. "Maybe," he said.

There was a marquee with pink and emerald bulbs and

tall letters that read: THE NEW TEXAS MOTEL—WE HAVE HOURLY RATES—XXX-PLUS MOVIES!

Raymond whipped on a pair of dictator-style dark glasses.

He wheeled into the central court for the motel, where parking slots surrounded a circle of chicken-wire fencing. Inside the fence, a couple lean boys reclined, sunbathing on lounge chairs.

Attached to the motel was a shack called The Anzac Club. In a box of shadows from the overhang of its tin roof three Mexican women swayed. They were all three stout women, all rocking to the cowboy music issuing from the club. A newborn baby gestured in the arms of the stoutest.

Raymond got out and went over to her.

I stayed in the green car.

He ambled back to me eventually, swinging a room key. "You wanna come with?" he asked.

"I guess I do," I said.

"Be sure now. You're not counting on anything."

I boosted off the mushy seat and stepped out of the convertible.

We entered the motel room through a rusted pummeled door that looked as though it'd been wrenched from its hinges and smashed in before.

Inside, a pinging air-conditioning unit kept the temperature icy and mixed up smells of people and disinfectant and a fruity incense.

The walls had new wood-tone paneling.

Mostly there was a bed—a swollen featherbed under a black velvet throw.

"Well, no husband," Raymond said. He turned to me. "Maybe you're glad."

"But he was here? *Here* here?"

"Afraid so. My Spanish is leaky but I believe she said last night, and they didn't none of them see him leave. But he's left," Raymond said.

He dropped onto the carpeting and got cross-legged. He popped on the TV.

The screen showed nude men with a slender woman, very busy.

"Good, the BBC," I said.

"Sorry. I just thought you oughta get the whole landscape."

"Oh," I said, "I know the landscape."

The show wasn't a movie, it was a video, and the moans and gasps that went with it sounded contained and local, as if coming from the next room.

"Well, look at that," I said.

"I don't wanna," said Raymond.

"She's made different from me."

"You better hope she is," he said. He put out the picture and his shoulders sagged.

I didn't move. My knees were crooked over the high edge of the bed and my bottom seemed to be sinking through the mattress, but I didn't get up, didn't let my gaze wander from the gray iridescence of the blank TV screen.

"Well," Raymond said. "We need us a telephone before we can go any fuh-thuh."

Back in the green convertible we drove an access road that paralleled the Gulf Freeway. We passed a furniture warehouse, industrial plants, a Flintkote factory that was sided with glazed tiles.

My motel room was at the Park Inn, a pricey building built during the boom.

The room had a low ceiling, and off the front balcony was a great palm that sent barbed shadows through the picture window and made pointy areas of darkness and chill.

Raymond docked his car next to my rental, the red Firecat.

"Don't think we're quitting yet," he said, as he stopped his engine from screaming.

Now instead we had the happy ratcheting of a zillion cicadas.

"There's still several of Raf's people I can ask. Who might've caught his act someplace or other."

In my room were pieces of blond rattan furniture. The quilted bedspread and cushions and carpeting were gray-green colors. Tropical-Confederate was the motif here, I supposed.

Raymond yanked off his heavy boots and kicked them that-away, dropped backward onto the bed, stacked both pillows behind his shoulders to prop himself up.

Over the dressing-room counter, I slit cellophane from a throw-away drinking tumbler but could draw only warm water.

Raymond steadied the gray desk phone on the lap of his jeans. He was all business, readying to make calls.

I went out for a bucket of ice.

On the room's far back wall were glass doors that could be jerked open to a catwalk and for a view of the court below. The court had a patio, web-and-metal lounge chairs, an Olympic pool, all-out landscaping.

I went with my tumbler of ice water through the sliding glass doors.

It was evening now, and a hundred artificial lights glowed on the court below. Down there were Black Southern Baptist goings-on.

The Park Inn was hosting a couple of conventions this week—the Baptists, who posed in maillots and swim trunks of sherbet colors on the pool's concrete patio, and a gathering of foreign scholars, bearded men and pale women in dresses.

In the water at the pool's shallow end, the children of both groups spanked up fans of splash.

There were spotlights on the spears and spikes of junglery overhead. Shadows made jagged stabbing lines across the patio chairs and table umbrellas.

"Well, fuck it," Raymond said after a call. "Now you see him, now you don't. There's still several people I can talk to, though."

I said, "They're getting up a water-polo game down in the pool. You want a drink? There's a bottle of Hennessy in my things somewhere."

"Just soda pop," Raymond said. "I'm recovered, they call it."

"How long?"

"Three years." He clawed at his hair.

"Then what you especially didn't need was a visit from my husband, Jack Daniels."

"Hell, I *like* the guy," Raymond said.

"I know," I said and I did. "You gotta like Raf."

———

Raymond brought a swimsuit from the trunk of the green convertible.

"Would you get tossed outa here if I was to put myself in that pool? I would dearly love to," he said.

"No, of course you should. You deserve at least that for all your trouble."

"I been enjoying myself, actually," he said.

"Is Luisa your wife? I noticed her name painted on the car."

Raymond made his smile. He said, "Two years now. Which was all of the original bargain. I married her on an arrangement, see. Her family's rich. They wanted her in the States. We got a little daughter, Maria, now though. So I'm feeling pretty lucky."

The roar from the Gulf Freeway was like thunderstorm wind and with it came blasts of cheetering night birds. These were tiny birds that zipped; flitting birds.

I had grabbed the last empty chaise. Raymond was in the water. Above, a breeze moved the mighty palms and they hissed like shaken pom-poms.

I fixed on a conversation the foreign scholars were having at a nearby table.

"Today, I'm happy. Things look a little better."

"The weather?" someone asked.

"No, I mean in my country. The military removed the state of emergency, so who can tell? Perhaps they fear the October elections."

A man with a Czech accent said, "It's better for us as well, but we don't forget what happened after Dubcek."

The roar from the Gulf Freeway hadn't quit—a hushing noise, like a river flowing over a low dam.

"I watched your new film, Bolo," said an American with a comic's quick delivery. "Are you crazy? I didn't understand one thing."

"Nothing you liked?"

Someone said: "Most ideas we have aren't ours. We just think we thought of them."

"Is that your idea or someone else's?" asked the American.

"Wait, wait, wait," the man named Bolo began.

"Uh oh," the American said. "Echolalia."

"So obvious," the Czech said and I heard his bored sigh.

"Example?" someone asked.

Raymond was swimming a careful sidestroke the length of the pool.

"Jiri," the Czech said, "that is not your firsthand knowledge."

"Letters from my father, the papers, yes. Reliable origins, I'm sure," a voice said.

Bolo said, "Various texts, but they congeal. If I were filming this, I'd include Amida's frock, her little radio playing Vivaldi. . . ."

"Scarlatti," the Czech said.

"We men, sitting a certain way, competing for her attentions . . ."

"Selection, no?" someone said. "What it means to be an artist."

"That is again, Jiri, not your idea but a received one," said the Czech.

I elbowed up and, dragging my chair behind me, moved away from the scholars. They were reminding me too much of Cambridge.

Raymond sharked the pool from edge to edge now, wriggling along the basin submerged. He did well in the water, although there seemed not enough of it for him.

He vaulted out, switched around so he was seated with his shins dangling over the cement ledge, his burnished back to me. "I'm ten years younger," he said without turning.

He knew I was watching *him*, though.

Raymond pulled his Levi's on over his soaked trunks and made three more calls.

"Jesu Christay," he said, banging the receiver. "We just can't get this old truck painted."

"Raf," I said.

"I mean, damn! He could be in Saskatchewan or in the next room," Raymond said. He braced his back on the headboard, finally squinting at me in my poolside outfit: a tank top and jeans hacked off high on the thigh. "Are you real skinny? Or am I just used to different?"

"My weight could be down."

"No, maybe that's how you all're supposed to look these days. Maybe Luisa should tighten it up a button or two."

"I'm probably too thin . . . haven't been eating much the last few weeks," I said.

"Hunger strike? Or'd the cook run off with Raf?"

"Raf *is* the cook, in fact," I said.

"Don't get scratchy with me, darlin'. I know marriage is sacred, even if yours has gone screwy. But I'll tell you true, I'm glad *I'm* not married to Raf. Was he embellishing or you really teach at Harvard?"

"I do but it's nothing hard," I said. "A lot of the time it's like being a camp counselor."

"Raf was bragging on you," Raymond said.

He lit a cigarette, still studying me. His hair was towel dried, tousled. "So, what's your uh—what do you teach?"

"Poetry. Writing it. Reading it some."

"Brr," Raymond said.

"Poetry forms especially," I said. "Fixed forms are my area and what I try to write."

"Publish any of it?"

"Four books." I nodded. "And I'm halfway through another. Well, maybe not halfway. Haven't got much done since Raf left, though I'm supposed to be writing full-time. I have a year's leave from teaching. June to next June. I got an arts grant bigger than my Harvard salary."

Raymond said, "The more I see you, the more I think it's a good skinny you are."

"What do we do now? I mean, about Raf," I asked.

"Oh, there's still some brick walls we can beat our heads against," said Raymond.

Before he left, he said, " 'How is the gold become dim,' Lamentations: four, one."

He said tomorrow I should try an address near Viet Nam Plaza, close to the downtown. "No, wait on that until I can take you," he said. "Or pack a rod, I most strongly advise."

And on, " 'I am the man that hath known affliction. . . . It was I whom he led . . . where no light is,' Lamentations: three, verse—don't remember." He left.

The Firecat had cream-colored seats, a radio-cassette and c.d. deck, smoked windows, burglar alarms, willful air conditioning.

But I was late getting started, having put off awakening till noon and then spent an hour with the street map just trying to figure a route to Viet Nam Plaza.

As I drove along the South Loop now in dusk's glow, the banking sun and rising moon were comically big, vermilion.

I exited where my map was marked with Lumolighter; piloted down a ramp, passed the Phan Dai Butcher Shop, and entered a hopeless ghetto.

The downtown buildings—banks and towers from before the crash—with their height and cool angles and slick panes, loomed close but unreal as Oz beside these junkyard streets.

Like a little bit of Saigon, this village was—Hau Dac Ti Place: bombed-out restaurants, shelled shops. The houses were lean-tos, and there wasn't one lawn.

My fingernail creased the street map balanced on my thigh. I needed to find Astro Ave.

The address Raymond had given me was for a converted filling station: a windowless building with CATFISH DEN painted along its forehead. Another sign read, BILLIARDS, WINE SET UPS, AIR COOLED! Razzle-dazzle lights spangled on a third sign out in the gravel parking lot. Most of the letters were bashed out on that sign. I couldn't guess what it said—L T QU STL Y HA.

The temperature was a hundred and seven. The air smelled of crude oil. It felt *wet* but there would be no rain, not here or anywhere else according to the headline of the *Chronicle.*

Actually, the address was for the place upstairs, which was a natural-wood box on stilts. The area beneath the box was filled with candy-colored car seats, parts of cars, two refrigerators, a Danish Modern couch.

The only way up was an unrailed flight of steps. But up there, life! In three windows buzzed noisy fans.

The woman who answered my knock said, "You're from Raymond?"

"I'm Paige. Mrs. Deveaux."

"Right, then I'm Jewels," the woman said. She was light-skinned, green-eyed, blonde, with the face shape and features of a Scandinavian. She wore a flowered kimono.

Her place smelled like a dinner party—as if she'd made canapés—and of the hot shortening and flour for pastry foods.

A television vibrated with a man singing "La Tremenda."

The window fans made everything that was loose swing or flutter.

"Grab a beer," Jewels said. Her accent was all Texas and her voice had rust in its depths.

"We gotta yell over the fans but I never did believe in air conditioning. You know? I think sweating's good for your pores—sweat *awl* the time and stay youthful. You wanna have dinner with me, sweets?"

"No thanks," I said, but accepted the lo-cal beer she passed to me.

I watched her fill a brown-freckled tortilla with beans and rice and green chili picante.

"Raymond didn't really explain why I was supposed to come here," I said. "I'm hunting for my husband. Maybe you know that already."

"How do you smoke and keep your skin so smooth?" she asked.

Over her head hung a door-sized Fuelex poster that showed a growling wolf. "HI OCTANE 93," the poster said.

She said, "You belong to Raf, I know."

Now she lay back on a couch the color of papaya.

On an end table, rows of giant novena candles squatted in glass containers big as thermos jugs. One black holder had a cobra on its side. Another was printed with "Iglesia Bisettra!" and the letters dripped blood. Others were painted with little portraits or figures of saints.

Jewels's bathroom door wore a wood cemetery cross that was wired around with fabric flowers, white and hot pink.

She swirled beer in her cheeks as if using mouthwash. She swallowed and said, "Raymond has gotten so damned *keerful*. I miss the old Raymond, isn't that terrible? When he drank? But I do. I almost wish he'd have a slip. These are strange times."

"What's Raymond being careful about?" I asked. "Do you know where my husband is?"

"I sorta do. He's with Julio. Julio's mine. He's a wonderful man."

"But do you know where Julio is either?"

"I sorta do," Jewels said. "He's with my sister. Raf and him're both with my sister Reba. Me and Reba are hairdressers for Nicole Roccio? You know Nicole's. They're all over town."

"I just got here," I said.

"We do that and help out our daddy some. Our daddy owns that bar downstairs you probably seen."

She said, "You look like you're gonna scream, Mrs. Deveaux."

"Paige," I said. "I need to find Raf. And this reminds me of those nightmares when you're moving in slow motion. Please go on. You were saying about Reba? Your husband, Julio?"

Jewels smiled and waved off the smoke from my cigarette, which was unnecessary. Her fans were pushing such a current her blond hair blew on end.

She said, "All right, it's like this. When Raymond threw Raf out, Raf called up Reba . . ."

"Of course, naturally."

"Well," Jewels said. "Raf doesn't have a lot of money."

"But he sure has friends."

"Hey, sweets, don't climb on *me*. I'm not in this. I got a set situation with Julio. You mind if I ask about something, though? I can't quite *feature* you with Raf."

I bit on that, gave Jewels an assenting nod. Finally I said, "We're a lot alike, have a lot in common. . . ."

"Yeah, I can see that. You're much too straight for the Raf *I* know."

"I meant underneath," I said. I really didn't want to try for words on what was between Raf and me.

"Sex?" Jewels said.

"That and everything. We need each other. Otherwise we can't feed or dress ourselves. We don't know what to think next."

"Oh," Jewels said, gesturing acceptance with her raised eyebrows.

Outside a tomcat squealed.

"So Raf came over and he collected Julio, and then as soon as Reba got off work, they all three went to The Anzac Club and the New Texas Motel."

"I've seen it."

"Don't it give you the *sicks*, that place? They were there awhile though, and then at Reba's, and today they're either coming here or going to Facinita or over the border."

"I hope you didn't mean that last."

"Wish I didn't," Jewels said.

With her kimono she wore slacks and padded white shoes, like nurses' shoes.

"Did you just get off work? When did you last talk to any of them?" I asked.

"Few hours ago. . . . I gotta take a bath," she said. "You're more'n welcome to wait here. They might come, who knows? Or you could try Facinita. It's a dance place for Hispanics? But you know what? I think you could pass. You're brown as toast. You'd get hit on but they got security, no big deal. You should wear a bra if you go."

"What if they decide on Mexico?"

Jewels shrugged and moved through the door with the flowered cemetery cross.

I heard a torrent of bathwater.

She came back and undressed while she chattered at me. I thought this could be an act of competition, that she felt close to Raf and wanted to show me what I was up against. Or maybe she was like a kid, treating me as a sister, never imagining a same-sex erotic context. Or she was ready for anybody, anytime.

"Raymond quote the Bible to you? That shit drives me lupo. He never used to, I'll tell you that," she was saying.

Anyway, she didn't make a bad show. The room was hot and she had the sheen of perspiration she wanted. Tattooed around her ankle was a fine-link chain in indigo ink. I couldn't guess her age—eighteen or thirty-five—either way.

I finished my beer and it felt like nothing.

"Raymond used to be the best non-Latino man I ever knew," Jewels said. "That's *when* he was drinking. Now between Luisa, and the church, and AA . . . They've made him a robot. What's the point of him even living?"

She vanished again, and suddenly I didn't mind being here. I cracked a second beer.

Jewels had lit a few of the novena candles, and the winds

from the wagging fans played with the candle flames, sending them sideways every five seconds.

I unbagged a pen and my poetry notebook. Just words, I listed at first, but then I got a start on a tercet. This tercet, if a student had submitted it to me, would've earned a low C.

I reeled over and whomped cheerily on the bathroom door. "Jewels! How's the water?"

She said, "I'm glad you waited. I can go to Facinita with you. I won't need no ride home and you'll feel better if you're *with* someone."

I wanted to go alone, though. I wanted to get drunker, go alone, and the hell with a bra.

"What'll we do, leave a note for Raf and them?"

"Good thinking," Jewels called. "In case they decide to crash-land."

"Do you have any more of that beer?" I asked her.

"Sí," she said. "In the kitchen in the fridge compartment. Then how 'bout soaping my back for me?"

"Not this month, Jewels. Sorry."

"Texans are very friendly. You oughta get more friendly, Paige."

"Do I still get the beer?" I asked.

She didn't answer. I heard the squeak of her bottom as she realigned herself in the tub.

"Jewels?"

"Just help your ole fuckin' self," she said.

Facinita had probably been a bowling alley. It was a long, low unmarked building behind an acre of parking lot lighted bright as noon by security floods. A strip of stubby palms like giant pineapples lined up along the base of the façade. Shiny loud cars were patrolling.

Jewels had come in a dress right for an afternoon bride—pastry white, crisp, lacy. Her lips and eyelids were painted purple. "*Muerte*—very sensual," she told me.

The dance crowd here was excited, extravagantly sharped up.

Inside, little lights flashed through cellophane red gel. The music was salsa; the floor bouncing full.

Jewels spoke quick, liquid Spanish, pretty to my ears. She knew everyone. She hooked a tall boy who wore a suit that glinted like minnows.

When he talked, I overheard the sound "Huh-reeba"— Jewels's sister.

"Well, goddamn. Bingo," Jewels shouted. "They're here somewhere!"

"Where are the bars?" I asked.

She winked; nodded left.

I saw Raf.

He was bent over, his nose and mouth in the dark mane of a girl twenty years younger than he. Whatever he was saying made the young woman smile, shake her head no, smile again.

His shirt collar was open by three buttons and the V of his chest was tan. He did look handsome in his way, in his loose black suit, although there was a badge-sized bruise on his left cheekbone below his glass eye, and he seemed far along in his drunk. Just moving back and forth along the bar he stumbled twice.

His good eye finally caught me watching, and after a beat came his smile.

I moved by slow inches through the crowd.

"Paige . . . *Buensima*. Someone said you might be in town."

I nodded once, yes; afraid to say anything, what my voice might give away.

"You must want a drink. This is . . . somebody," he said, and the girl with the dark mane looked as though her arm were being bent out of socket.

"And this is uh . . . an old friend of mine, Julio," Raf said.

Julio had on a cowboy hat, and he held a thin umber cigar in his fingers. He pursed his lips at me, kissed three times.

"So, Paige," Raf said. "A drink?"

"Not now, thanks. Could we . . . ?"

"I must decamp," he told the dark-haired girl.

"Did our tanker come in? Is this *our* car?" he asked me. We had walked out into Facinita's yellow parking lot.

"It's just a rental," I said. "Raf?"

"A rental," he said and spat on the car.

I asked, "How bad off are you?"

He gripped my shoulders, backed me up against the door. I had one hand full of keys, the other opened on his chest, ready to shove him.

"Can you say how you *are* exactly?" I said.

He pressed into me, kissing my throat, my collarbone.

"I'm O.K.," he said. "Me? I'm . . . you know."

I drove on shut-down streets.

Raf liked the car's stereo and liked stamping the control tabs for the radio. He was doing this now with the toe of his shoe as he sipped bourbon from a silver flask.

I recognized a bridge that spanned Bray's Bayou and pulled off into what I thought was a public park. It was a cemetery.

"Uh oh," Raf said.

"Mind if we do without the radio for a minute?" I asked him.

"Here's where I get mine," he said.

"What happened to your face?" I asked.

He shrugged. "Keep falling down. You know, I read there's a once-in-a-millennium order of the sun and moon and all the planets of our . . . um . . . solar thing going on. Which could account for my imbalances, some of 'em."

We were under high trees that were bearded with ashen moss. Raf lit a cigarette, shutting his good eye to the burst of flame. The hot night was talking—crickets or frogs or sighing snakes—I didn't know.

"You're too thin," he said.

"Umm," I said.

His head dropped back on the car seat and he closed his eyes and smoked.

I studied his profile.

"Who's Jewels?" I asked, just to keep him conscious.

"Nobody."

"A friend? A toss?"

"Neither of those. Or not so's I committed to memory."

We were by a grove of banyans, yucca, drooping St. Agnes bushes.

Cozying up to the cemetery was a business line of gravestones with mirrory marble surfaces.

Raf pointed the glowing end of his cigarette at them. "Soon," he said. "My face and numbers, going right there."

"No. You've been having one long party, is all," I said.

"I missed you," he said. "Genuinely did. You know, someplace, not too many cities back . . . Somewhere I was at a zoo."

I said, "Then what happened? They let you out?"

"Just listen. I'm serious. They had a . . . Not a cage, but

a glass room . . . tiny. For this cheetah. She was sleeping in there with this rawhide bone—great big, femur-sized. Laid out, sleeping on the cement floor with her paws up under her chin. Finest thing I've ever seen. I can't stop thinking about it. My mind just goes there and stays."

I took a swallow from Raf's silver flask and got hot straight bourbon, an eye crosser.

"You wanted to get inside the room and play with the cat?"

"No, no, just watching her sleep. She was twitching, her eyes moving, like she was having a *dream*. Feet flexing. Dreaming of hunting probably. You should've seen it."

"How do you like Houston, Raf?"

He backhanded his jaw, making a brushing sound on his rough cheek. He took a second to think. He said, "Well, Paige, I don't *like* Houston."

"Because I have to go," I said. "Have to leave day after tomorrow. I was hoping you'd go back with me."

He pounded his clenched fist a couple times on the dash. "Well, probably should, but . . . you know me, how it goes with me. I'll get back up, be better 'n ever."

"I know," I said. "But *I* have to go. This's the last train out, I'm saying."

Now he bashed his palm on the dash. "*I can't fuckin' think,*" he said.

A bandy-legged Asian groundskeeper was doing night work of some kind, laboring over by the roses near the main gates. He wore a platterlike hat. I watched him instead of looking at Raf, who was saying, "I am too old for the constant fuckin'. . . . One uncomplicated dream is all I ask. How could I think about going back with you? That seems so blessedly long ago I lived in the motherfucking East."

"So, no?"

He sighed. "Gimme a little time. Christ fuck, Paige, give me a *night* before I decide."

I thought of the Countess in *The Marriage of Figaro*, when she sings, "I am kinder: I will say yes," and lets her husband off for so much everything that the chorus blasts, "Then let us all be happy!"

"I've got a motel room," I told Raf. "Olympic pool, room service, all that shit."

As we were merging into traffic on the Loop, Raf said, "You probably don't wanna go back and gather up some of my friends. I'm just axin'."

I said I wouldn't mind going to fetch Raymond Hollander.

"Oh, you met Raymond, huh?"

"I'll say I did."

"There's a bad story there. I'll tell it to you sometime. I'm not the hero of the piece."

We were into the stream of cars now.

"Such a surprise," I said.

In blackness, the instant the room door clicked shut, I heard Raf open his zipper.

"What do I know, but you seem too messed up." I snapped on a lamp with a pleated shade.

"Yeah, I'm wrecked," he said. "And yet, it's funny. I look down and I've got this potato pointing at you. If that's not funny, well then, I've been reading all the wrong philosophers."

He collapsed against the wall in a corner of the room and was sliding. When he reached the sculpted floor carpeting, he said, "Aw, hell."

"We should get some solid food for you, Raf. And I have B vitamins that you ought to take, so you can think."

"You got it all wrong. I can't fuckin' *stop* thinking. The horror show runs all the time now."

"I know. That's what I mean. So you can think well and clear again."

"I got clear thoughts on you," he said.

"Aw, thanks," I said. "You can show me sometime when you're really here. When it's really *Raf* I'm talking to."

He stopped me with a look, fierce and sudden and serious, his glass eye sending furious points of light. "You're talking to me, Paige."

"And who might you be these days?"

"Another dying animal," he said with a shrug.

"Back on the death thing, huh?" I said, but his eyes dropped.

And there he was in the corner, his dark figure stretched out, his face stilled, sleeping.

The bureau lamp's pleated shade made harsh darting light shapes so I angled it to shine on an empty niche, and switched on the soft track lights bordering the wall high above the bed.

I padded around barefoot, in and out of the shower, emerging at last with a skimpy motel towel safety-pinned like a mini sarong.

All I wanted was Raf conscious, but I didn't try waking him. I thought about lying beside him on the floor.

Instead I flumped onto the jumbo bed and pulled magazines from my rope tote bag—*Granta*, an *American Poetry Review*, an issue of *Zoom*.

"Don't ask me about Raymond Hollander," Raf said from the corner.

"No, I wasn't going to. I left you for dead over there, old son."

"I Lazarused. That's been happening lately, just when I'm really enjoying being dead."

"Oh, stay on the fucking floor," I said.

"Too late," Raf said.

I glanced around my magazine.

He was having great difficulty scaling the bed. He was hauling himself by his arms and hands, as if climbing from a diving pool.

He lost hold and fell out of sight.

"Come on, up and over," I said. "You can do it."

He stripped off his jacket and T-shirt, and lunged onto the mattress, landing beside my legs.

"Well, that was almost," I said.

Raf said, "*This* is the moment all those grueling months of *training* were for."

"That's right."

"The hours on the practice mattress . . . The work on technique . . . All that is over. Right now, right here, it's just a question of pride and character; a question of will."

It was one of Raf's better nights. He was ambitious and strong, which surprised me, and it surprised me that he could carry through.

THE CHURCH OF
SUN AND FLOWERS

AT DAWN I pulled on a swimsuit and crept down to the pool court.

The gulf air was warm and there were breakfast smells from the restaurant, and the chlorine-clean odor of the blue-green water, and there were tree and leaf smells as well.

The surface of the lighted pool wobbled and glistened.

I dozed on a lounge chair and dreamt in bolts and bursts of neon color. I awoke excited by the escalating heat.

Maybe it was ten.

Trundling past me on this side was a maid with a loaded utility cart.

On my other side was Raf, a morning cup of bourbon balanced on his open hand. He held the cup forward, offering me a taste.

Beside him was a shrub with leaves like bayonets.

I said, "Houston, right? The world, third planet from the sun? Not just that I read too much Beckett?"

"Paints up your dreams," Raf said.

"Intensely. How did you know that?"

He sipped his bourbon, shrugged. "Your dreams are same as mine, Paige."

"No, hardly. Well, O.K., yeah, sure. Some, maybe."

Raf said, "A house with a well-kept yard, two boys . . ."

"Lyle and Vartimin," I said for him. "Lyle has a red wagon, a paper route. Vartimin has a complexion problem and also a weight problem—he needs to reduce—but he's an awfully nice fellow. These were really vibrant shades in my dream. I didn't know my mind could *du*plicate such color."

"Umm," said Raf. "That's Houston."

I reminded him I'd once gone very far away, where everything was different, every rule changed.

"Africa, yeah, but you'd had your shots."

"Where's the farthest you've been?" I asked.

He looked at me, thinking. "South Pole."

"Oh, of course, the South Pole." I shook my head. "And I'll never know if that's true. No way to know."

For lunch, Raf chose a Mexican restaurant with rough plank benches. On the walls hung acrylic paintings and straw dolls. There were potted cacti.

He dug some Pacifico beers from a bin of cubed ice and gulped those while I ate hot flour tortillas, scoops of guacamole and sour cream.

When he'd finished his beers, Raf managed a few bites of chicken in chocolate sauce, two spoonfuls of black bean soup.

"Now what happens?" I said.

"You mean we're all done fucking around, Paige?" he said.

There was music from overhead: a plinking guitar and swaying fiddles.

"Why did you leave me, Raf?"

Behind the fiddle sounds, the guitar was doing something like high math.

"I wasn't leaving you," he said. "I had to see Raymond's why I ended up here. He's helped me before; scraped me off a couple other walls."

"How? Who *is* he?"

"Old friend. We were schoolmates."

"Oh, uh huh. Was that at Princeton or when you were reading at Oxford? Don't even tell me, I don't want to hear."

"Cute girl behind the counter," Raf said eventually.

She had been cute when we pushed through the entrance door and she was cute now. She had a nice back and her stupid dress showed all of it.

"Everything a boy could want," I said and sighed.

Raf let smoke trail from his mouth.

Because of his glass eye, his gaze could go off in two directions and someone confronting him who wasn't used to this had to guess.

But I knew where Raf was focused. His quiet smile was aimed at me while his working eye worked over the bared back of the counter girl.

We drove out an eight-lane highway—the Old Spanish Trail, it was called—toward the Astrodome. I saw L.A.–type blight: Wal-Marts, a thousand fast fooderies, convenience stores.

A bank sign eighty feet aloft flashed us the temperature in computer digitals: 103° F.

"Turn up here," Raf told me.

Now we were passing grand homes with deep shade and broad lawns of jewel-green Bermuda grass.

"Next block, go right, on through the iron gates," he said.

We rode a meandering drive on the grounds of a Catholic convent. Shadows splattered everywhere over the yards and banks of flowers. There were white statues, luminous on their pedestals.

The radio's weather announcer said hurricane winds were hammering the Grenadines, that a thunderstorm was drenching the Panhandle.

Where we were, though—before the brick convent building—curtains of bright rain fell. The sun was out, but the rain came down as if thrown from lawn sprinklers.

Raf said, "Let me just light this cigarette."

An Archangel Michael, twice life-sized, stood guardian before the convent's door. I watched a nun in a blue dress and hood as she went running for him.

And I saw a tiny orange-and-yellow lizard flicker up a cottonwood tree.

Raf inhaled and said, "Now. I swear to you, before God here and all his angels and virgins and shit, that I mean to clean up, dry out . . ."

"Before or after you go back with me?" I asked.

"Uh, go back with you. Before. It'd have to be before. But, so, that's my plan, those are they, so help me. Loyola."

"How long will all this take?"

"Don't ask me that, Paige."

From the elementary school next to the Catholic convent came sixty Mexican girls—in box-pleated skirts and white uniform blouses—who moved, holding hands, in a two-by-two line.

Raf took more bangs of bourbon from his silver flask;

offered it to me. His glass eye was closed while the other feasted on the summer schoolers.

"You don't know quit," I said to him.

"I was just trying to imagine you decked out like that."

"Twelve idiot years of my life."

"With the ribbon-in-the-hair deal?"

"Sure, the ribbon."

"Turn at the corner. There's something you gotta see," Raf said.

"Is it a museum, Raffles? Or a gallery? I know Houston has like the Menil Collection and the Rothko Chapel. And fine-arts museums with couches and guides and gift shops."

He was punishing the radio again, shoving in its buttons with a knuckle, twisting its dials. He tuned in a Caribbean station, a show featuring the Rastafarian Brigadier Gerry the General, and kept ahead of Gerry singing "Hafta Get a Beatin'."

I nibbled a red licorice stick from a bag that had ridden on the car's back seat since being plucked from a wire carousel at Hobby Airport.

Now Raf was directing me along avenues of shanties and weed lots, up Jessamine, Delphine, El Camino.

We paused at the railway crossing for seven passing blue-and-yellow Santa Fe switch engines. I said, "Don't laugh, but I sort of like watching trains. I and every other American."

"I don't think being normal's your worry," Raf said.

My window was down. The air felt sticky, as before a hard rain. The sky had purpled up in the rearview, readying for a storm burst.

"Don't let this get to you, this last. You don't ever have to come back here," Raf said.

We were into a Hispanic neighborhood. "Clinica, Albierto Todos Los Dias Del Anos," I read from a sign.

"Turn up there—not quite a road," he said.

It was more of a trail, jagged, with plates of old blacktop and asphalt that rocked the car and bounced us as we crossed. One pothole was like a Ferris wheel drop. It jerked the radio song out of a phrase or so.

"Slow up. This whole section's one of the worst wards," Raf said.

There was a gathering of little girls with thick hair braids, baggy clothes, white anklets and huaraches who shouted something in Spanish as we passed.

"See that shack?" Raf said, turning in his seat. He meant a cinderblock hut. Its bubble-gum-pink paint was sun-faded. Kids' bikes with banana-shaped seats were angled around the shack, lying down or leaning on their kick-stands.

"O.K., yeah, I do," I said.

"It's the sniff house of choice. Bigger than it looks. Most popular," Raf said.

"Oh."

He said, "Kids can do glue or aerosols or shine in there. They come out pretty goofy."

"I don't thank you for showing me this," I said. "And probably the Chamber of Commerce is smart not to mention it in the tour catalogue."

"Keep going," Raf said. "On up to that parking lot."

The lot stretched out behind a movie theater named The Lido Six. Abandoned trash dumpsters, filled and fenced over with kudzu, blocked the theater's rear-exit doors.

"You go through those doors into the theater and inside . . ."

"*I* don't go through those doors," I said, gunning out of the lot. The tires made static noises crossing the lot.

Broken glass was strewn everywhere; glass ground fine as rock salt.

"No, but I have," Raf said. "And inside is the Church of Sun and Flowers. There's a room in the basement with twenty or thirty people sitting around in the dark. Some have been there for days, weeks; they *never* want to leave."

A blond bundle like a long duffel bag lay ahead in the cement road.

"Is this a dead man?" I asked Raf. I slowed the car and closed my eyes. "I'm sure he's dead. He looks rumbled over by trucks. We have to do something."

"Stop when you get to him, but keep the motor running," Raf said.

He kicked open his door and leaned out over the figure. "Umm, he's not dead. He's resting."

I clunked the car into gear and drove. On Dahlia, we passed a clutch of sick-looking boys in ponchos and felt hats.

"They been to the movies," Raf said. "Now, you wanna go to the MFA?"

"No, I'm out of the mood. What I really want to do is get into the fetal position and suck my thumb."

"Yeah, I know. Especially when you figure that's eighty percent of the fuckin' world. The palace is surrounded," he said. "The serfs are plenty pissed."

"I haven't asked what errand took *you* into that theater-church place."

"No, and don't," he said, tapping out the last drink from his flask.

We went by a boarded-up nightclub and a boarded-up cabana, both behind razor-wire fencing. "Trevino Bail Bonds" was the cabana's business. The nightclub had a sun-whitened sign that read: "GIRLS! GIRLS! GIRLS!"

"Where Pru used to work," Raf said.

"Something else I will never ever ask about," I said.

We sat on café chairs at a little table in a club called The Yellow Man. Raf had skinned off his shirt and wore only his black jeans. His tanned bare chest was damp, as the bar had a couple floor fans but no real air conditioning.

He was watching me now, even as he tipped the iced bourbon in his grip. He laid his left boot on my lap.

For something to do, I pretended I was a radio. I figured Raf could listen or not.

I talked about my Grandpa Amelio, how he had converted his barn and smokehouse and the heavy-equipment garages into studios for the sculptures he and my father did: civic sculptures—statues, monuments; and park stuff—equestrian statuary, Civil War, and Lafayette. I mentioned that my grandfather, by the time he died, had done eight George Washingtons, three on horseback.

A man interrupted me—a chubby, white, curly-haired college-aged man—to beg a dollar for a drink.

"Let go of her shoulder, Greg. Billy!" Raf called to the bartender. "Two for Greg, but over there."

The Greg man bustled away. The other half-dozen patrons of The Yellow Man were Caribbeans, men and women who knew Raf well enough to greet him by name and leave him alone.

I went on talking family history. I told about roaming the sculpture barn when I was little, wandering among horses' heads that were taller than I, and huge faces of presidents and statesmen.

"I had a wood-burning kit," Raf said.

I said my father and grandfather worked twelve-hour

shifts when they had a job, until gradually, out of the rock, a shape would appear. And it was sad, I told Raf, to see some of them go. "So we'd have a goodbye dinner; a farewell to the Allegorical Figure of Justice, or to Roger Taney, or to the Symbol of Athletic Competitive Spirit for the University of Eastern Maine."

"My dad worked as a salesman," Raf said.

"Then in the end, you know," I said. "They'd use the statue for maybe the top of the train station in Wilmington or Iowa City. And there it'd be, up with the clouds."

"Mom hooked rugs," Raf said. "There they'd be, right underfoot."

I went on to how Mario, my father, had *stopped* making monuments in the sixties when the market dried up and there were no commissions. "Nobody wanted eagles on freeway bridges anymore. But we should go to Brigham Park in Philly sometime, Raf."

"It tops off my dream vacation list," he said.

"No, listen," I said. "When I was twelve or thirteen, Mario got his final commission and it was for a bronze water sprite for this marble fountain in Brigham Park. And he used *me* as his model."

"Aw, come on, when you were twelve, Paige? Are you sure?"

"Of course I'm sure, I remember it exactly. I mean, modeling nude. . . . And Mario—opera roaring away on the phonograph—in his apron and goggles. I think he was just so frustrated by failure he wanted to spit in the eye of propriety. As if to say, 'Fine, you want jigsaw puzzles and car wrecks for your sculptures? And turn your backs on Michelangelo and the Greeks and three thousand years of figurative art? Well, here's what you'll be missing.' "

"He sure never mentioned this to me," Raf said. "Jesus. His own daughter."

"Well," I said, "whose *other* kid was he going to get?"

"I can't judge the man," Raf said. His voice was scratchy and low from drink now.

Through the doorway and windows came a brown-orange light that meant sunset. And over the sweet scent of Raf's bourbon I could smell palm, and a flinty odor from fireworks the neighborhood kids had set off.

Dawn, and I came awake as if falling from a great height; falling from somewhere hot, white, hectic with the sounds of screaming machinery.

My one leg was tangled up with Raf's.

I found nothing hot or white in the motel suite, nothing noisy going on, but pulling loose from Raf I saw the angles of his cheekbones and jaw and the line of his brow looking sharp and starved and terribly dark and beautiful against the bedding, and suddenly I had no patience for empty time, plotless hours, quiet.

Room service brought up a carafe of coffee. While cold water streamed into the bath, I printed words in my poetry notebook:

Live Oak Drive
Lido Six
saffron
Cujaness
rispetto
the summer with all the falling stars
Palo Pinto

baby lizard—detailed, nectarine orange-yellow
    body, thread of vein on belly, silver and lavender
    eye stains

San Saba
island lace
black gum on saloon floor
crystalwood
pin nails
hackberry
rain on the convent grounds
the Chickanut Sewing Circle

I phoned my mother at the seaside inn she managed. Eastern time, it would've been about eight.

"Oh, thank God," Dottie said.

I pictured her in a dressing gown, her pretty legs bare, her feet half tucked into mules, sitting on the side of the bed in the Commodore's Suite, her hand pressed to her chest in relief. She adored Raf.

"Your father lit a candle to—I think—Saint Anthony," she said. "Whoever's the patron or angel in charge of lost and found."

"Yes, well, Saint Anthony can't grab all the credit. I get some."

"I'm sure it was an anguished search," my mother said.

"Wait a second, Mother. How would you know anything about Dad?"

Dottie squirreled out of answering me.

My parents had been divorced twenty years.

Someone tapped on the window sill. I notched the chain and cracked the door open on Raymond.

"Raymond?" I said.

"King of the cowboys. I decided to duck work today.

D'I wake you? You're still in your bathrobe. Guess it's only seven something."

I let him inside.

"You found the loathsome one," he said.

The sleeves of his shirt were rolled on his brown arms. He looked sun-tinged and he seemed more inhabited than he had before.

We stood uneasily, both staring at Raf.

"Say what you will, that boy can surely sleep," Raymond said. "I gotta make a smoke run. You care to ride along?"

We took the Firecat, which Raymond wanted to drive.

"Well, I'm glad you caught up with him. How awful was it?" he asked me.

"I suppose it could've been a happier reunion, but at least he wasn't bumping anybody at the time," I said, and saw Raymond wince.

"I should be more careful with my phrasing," I said.

"Whew," said Raymond.

"It was nice of you to fall by."

"No," he said, "it wasn't."

He drove under the Loop into West University—a leafy neighborhood of old brick homes. The yards here were mostly rust-colored soil, but where there was grass it appeared a livid green.

"Magnolia Street," Raymond said. "See that house with the arch?"

He meant a tidy one-story where a shadowed front porch had, strung under its arch, an empty parakeet cage.

"Woman lived there worked for my family for twenty years. Ida Consuela Nightingale. Half black, half Mex. She died just a year back."

"Nightingale?"

"Ugly as her name was beautiful," he said. "But her old man Harold loved her like life and breath. Harold's probably inside there now, mourning. You know there wasn't a day he didn't deliver her to us. And then he'd *be* there to collect her. Always a little early. He didn't want her on no bus and didn't trust her to a cab, so he'd take time off work to chauffeur her. Forty-some years of marriage and they never were apart, except for their jobs. I kinda think that's *it*, don't you? The thing itself."

"Oh, I wouldn't know, Raymond."

"Well, I would," he said.

He pointed at a checkerboard place with a neon script sign: "The Panaderia."

"Best bakery in Houston. But back on what I was saying, what *I* want is like that, and nothing less. I don't see the *sense* of anything less."

We shared the last cigarette in his pack, taking puffs and passing it to each other.

Over a closed dry cleaner's, on a plywood sheet, nineteen worn Michael Jackson posters were pasted. They were black and white with life-sized figures of Michael Jackson, and in splashing red "BAD" was printed nineteen times.

Vivaldi, my father had listened to. And Scarlatti and Handel. Bach, of course. Those composers had gone right with the magnitude of Mario's sculptures.

Everything with him was hard and deductive and serious, but inflamed.

We glided into the lot of a fuel station–convenience store called the T-EX.

In its tiny yard, in the morning sun, stood a lovely girl. She was maybe fourteen, heavily pregnant. She wore a maternity frock of lime-colored cotton.

Raymond let the engine idle and kept on the air conditioner. Turning to me, he said, "Can I ask you something real personal, Paige?"

I nodded.

He pushed his dark dictator glasses up the bridge of his nose. "I don't know, am I rilly weird? Because I can have sex with strangers just fine. I acquit myself just fine. But if I get to know her, even a squinch . . ."

"You're not weird," I said.

"Well, that's all about what?"

"I think only a stranger can have magic. Maybe that's why your spouse can't hypnotize you. Or anyone in your family, or any good friend. . . . And probably another reason's fidelity. As if you aren't really being unfaithful with a stranger—she's just a body, just a female."

"That's a sweet view, darlin'. I bring all this up 'cause of Raf, actually."

"How's that?"

"He's same as me. Now and then, he just reaches and takes whatever's there," Raymond said. "But it doesn't mean a thing to him. 'Course you know that, or you wouldn't stick by. I'd sure hate to see it if you weren't sticking. The guy'd go straight down in flames. You think he's fucked up now, well, I seen him plenty more fucked, in the old days, before you."

I told Raymond there was no chance of my saving Raf, but that I wouldn't want to do without him, despite reaching and taking.

A sedan slid up next to us. Its driver wore a sleeveless black T-shirt and had a sprayed and set haircut with a wave cresting off his forehead. Around his rearview mirror he'd strung a pair of red nylon panties.

"What did you and Raf fight about?" I asked. "He didn't—not Luisa."

Raymond said, "I try to convince myself it wasn't Raf. Didn't *do* anything but he was brimming over with suggestions."

"I am awfully sorry to hear that."

"It's O.K. Other night at the motel room with you . . . and I don't have the excuse of bein' drunk and despondent."

"But what?" I said. "I'm not a complete stranger, so you didn't try anything?"

"I didn't," Raymond said, unwhapping his seat belt and moving on the seat to face me, "only because you were so strung out about Raf. You should know that, and maybe *he* should, in case he ever sobers up and starts thinking too poorly of himself."

Climbing out, the young man with the fancy haircut binged our car door with his own.

"Hey, Pablo, watch it there," Raymond said.

A wind from nowhere leaned on the odd trees around the T-EX, combed the grass in the tiny yard, flattened stands of sun-crisped wild flowers.

I zipped down my window. This wind felt hot. The north sky was plum. Overhead, the sky had gone cobalt and there were brushstroke clouds, furry clouds.

I said hi to the pregnant girl in lime green. Her arms were folded above her big stomach and she was walking, aimlessly it seemed, up and down the yard.

Raymond swung out of the store now, clutching an unbagged carton of True Blues and a webbed six-pack of diet sodas. There was a snap to his hips as he walked. He had no more waist than I and he carried a lot of shoulder. The sun shone on his blond, metal-bright hair. I hadn't seen anything quite so good on the hoof since the diving pool lifeguard when I was sixteen.

I considered the next car—the guy's red underpants trophy; and the pregnant *child* roaming the T-EX yard there. I decided the rank steam heat of this city must knock its people sideways.

Riding back, Raymond said, "That was exaggeration about Harold and Ida Nightingale. You believe everything, don't you?"

"Down here I do. You mean that wasn't true?"

"Four-eighths true." He bit the sealing strip of cellophane from a fresh cigarette pack. "I was makin' a point," he said.

He said, "You know what Raf was doing when I first met him?"

"Uh, guessing could take a while."

"It was weird. Weirdest. We were both on the freshman squad there at Princeton. . . ."

"You really were at Princeton? I mean, Raf told me that. . . ."

"But you didn't believe it. Football," Raymond said. "They didn't give athletic scholarships in the Ivy, but they could make things plenty easy for a good linebacker and I *was* that. 'Course then my pa was an alum, and there's recruitment quotas—like they gotta have a certain number from the Southwest and so forth."

"Still," I said. "You must've been a pretty sharp tack."

Raymond said, "And I was only there two years 'fore they booted my butt out. But so here's Raf and me and we're the stars of the freshman team, so we buddied up."

Raindrops appeared on the windshield and wriggled down in zigzag patterns. Raymond got the wipers clicking.

"So our teammates there had money to throw away, some of them. And what Raf'd do was draw pictures for 'em, for pay."

"I've heard about this," I said.

"Guy would say, 'Draw me a chick,' and Raf would do it, real as any photograph. And the guy'd say, 'Longer legs,' so Raf would just erase and make changes. And then the guy would say, 'Now draw another chick on *top* of her.' And Raf would tell him, 'That'll cost an extra five, you know?' "

"A commercial artist," I said.

"Or like a cop sketch artist, only for the perverted. Guy would say, 'Make her ass wider and put in a dog.' And Raf would look real worried and he'd say, 'A dog. That'll be *twenty* more. They're hard!' "

We drove. Raymond wagged his head and smiled. He said, "Raf could draw anything you wanted."

"I'm so proud of him," I said.

At a stoplight we heard a siren throbbing and Raymond pushed his hand between my legs.

"This is a different record you're playing," I said.

"No," Raymond said. "It's the flip side of the same."

Back at the motel, Raf seemed only murkily aware of us.

A car-wreck movie played on the jumbo color television. The movie had a wet-lipped stripper, shiny with sweat, strolling a shiny runway in a shiny saloon.

Raf told me my legs were better than hers.

"I think she's a man," Raymond said.

Raf said, "Paige's a man? You been hanging out in the wrong restrooms, *amigo*."

"The film person there is a man," said Raymond.

I agreed with him. "That's a guy, Raf. And still *his* legs are better than mine."

"Wicked world," Raf said.

Raymond said, "Well, I'll be off. But if you're around tomorrow, Paige, and if you feel up to it, Raf, I'm driving over to see the Consul General of Mexico. Cónsul Hen-e-rail du Meh-he-co."

"Give him a blow job," Raf said.

"Might turn out that way. You know that amnesty deal for illegal aliens?"

"Don't trust that shit. It's a trick to deport some and skin the others for back taxes," Raf said.

"Luisa's got a brother who might qualify if there's still time. I'm gonna find out—no *names* named. You all wanna come along, you're most welcome."

"Tempting," I said.

"Afterwards, I was gonna take you to lunch," Raymond said. " 'Cause see the consulate's over in the fag-museum-boutique area they call the Montrose district."

"Raf won't go if there's no horse manure for him to toss around in," I said.

"Yeah," Raf said. "True. It's not an authentic day for me unless I degrade myself in so many ways."

I dreamt Raf lay beside me in a cold room. I dreamt a freak snowstorm had fallen and left a snowy pudding on the floor and I was thirsty. Someone caressed me, and I liked the caress, but explained, "Wait, wait. I need water first."

I came to at four a.m. and heard the wenk-wenk of my wristwatch. I unbuckled the strap and flung the watch at the sliding glass doors.

"What'd you do that for, Paige?" Raf asked me. He was awake.

"The *sound*," I said.

"Hey, hey," he said. "Easy. It's just another night."

Later I left the bed and Raf—who sat now, still awake; slapping through my copy of *Zoom*—to drink all the tap water my body would hold.

Sunrise lured me, barefoot and in my bathrobe, out onto the front balcony.

The sky had heat lightning. Quick sequences of it strobed the grape clouds.

A black woman in a pale linen suit came from the next suite and stood watching *with* me, as though I'd been expecting her.

Over the way, we could see the Southern Cross Nursery with its banner: LINERS SHRUBS GROUND COVER & TREES. We could see a freight truck garage bleached of color by the security lights yet burning. Not much else, though, in view.

The woman spoke with an accent. She asked if I smelled rain. I didn't.

She said, "I lost a friend a while ah-go." She stroked her cheeks as if to exercise some change on herself. "So I pace, not sleeping. And ahm enticed into stupid thoughts about destiny. Cynical as we are, we could say something for it, I suppose."

The sky blinked with a spear of lightning, followed by a boom.

She said, "This man I won't bore you about, in Trinidad,

he lost a testicle in surgery. Nothing could have mattered less to me. But he never came to believe me on that. And what does his affliction mattah now? Not at all."

The motel door stood ajar and I could see that back in the room the TV—soundless, but showing a film—made everything in there gold, now blue, now circus red.

The woman was silent until she came up with this: "A mile or so that way is a self-serve carwash. They have vacuum hoses. You can clean the seats, do the inside, wash the exterior and dry it. Mine is the white Jetta. I think that ees what I will do, and feel better after."

Raymond collected me around noon.

He drove across town, along Telephone Road, the Martin Luther King Highway, Navigation Boulevard, and into a dandified neighborhood of southwestern art deco, Miami-ish palms, stucco and glass-block condos, dappled ponds of shade. The storm had well passed and straight overhead the sun was white. Everywhere, I heard the twitch and sputter of lawn sprinklers.

A collie dog ambled across the parkway ahead of the car.

"Yep," Raymond said, grinning at the dog.

The Mexican Consulate had the ground floor of a six-story amber-glass-and-concrete box.

"This won't be but ten or fifteen hours," Raymond said. "Then I'll take you to some rum ordinary."

He was in a blousy white shirt and a tie but wore his wash-faded Levi's.

I drifted around the immaculate lobby. It was spacious, somber, chilled. There were desert saguaros in earthen pots, and some bland abstract wall paintings I spent time on.

I wandered out into the sunny lot, where Mexican flags flapped high overhead—green, red, and white.

Across the street, whole families squeezed under an awning at a place advertising "Passport Photos, Immigration, Fingerprints—FOTOS de MEXICO."

Too near me, a bird landed on its own shadow. This was an eerie bird, white-eyed. I moved away from it to a glen of shade.

There was a glitzy house opposite where I stood. Before the house were willows and a hand-painted sign for twenty-four-hour palm readings with "Sister Andros."

I walked over. Inside the bright living room a tiny woman wearing pink sneakers sat in an armchair and frowned at a tumbler of fizzing yellow seltzer she held.

"You again," she said.

"Me? I've never been here before."

"Then your twin has," the woman said.

"I don't have a twin. I was an only child. Are you Sister Andros?"

"Who wants to know?"

"Never mind," I said. "I just came over here to kill time."

"What I meant is we're closed," Sister Andros said.

"On your sign it says open twenty-four hours."

The woman gently fingered her head. "It's not you," she said, "it's this headache. Some other time?"

Back in the cool lobby of the Consul General's offices, I got cross-legged on the marble floor and stared at a great cactus posted in a clay drum.

Raymond was the only blond in line; easy to spot. He stood at the head now, chatting with a chic woman on the business side of the desk.

I liked watching Raymond and realized as he sauntered

over to me that I felt contented in the cool and wished he'd taken longer.

"Is that it? Everything's settled already?" I asked.

"Mostly, if you can trust 'em. They wanted specifics and I kept it all hypothetical, but just *filing* costs you."

I said, "Raymond, you're friends with Luisa's brother? You want him living with you?"

He looked confused. "More the merrier, ain't it?"

Back at the motel suite, Raf, covered only by a waist-knotted towel, was pacing at a mean tempo, incensed, distressed, fearful; maybe all those. He seemed sober, but I could seldom be sure. He had plenty of talent for camouflaging drunkenness.

"Maids want fucking *in* here," he said.

"They want fucking in here? So where's your problem?" said Raymond.

"Hi, Raymond," Raf said, dropping onto a chair.

"Oh, are we gonna be friendly?" Raymond asked.

I rang the desk and canceled housekeeping services for the day.

Raf said, "I need support before I do what I gotta do."

"Get dressed?" Raymond asked him.

"No, a shower."

"Oh, the *heavy* work," Raymond said.

"I'm a hero in my book," said Raf. "If you two hear dying noises . . ."

A bourbon scent mixed with the hot cloud from Raf's bath.

Outside, rush hour. The motel was filling up. There were traffic noises, and the sounds of car doors and trunks being slammed, the voices of guests unloading luggage, bringing luggage up the stairs.

Raf's black Levi's were half zipped. He was shirtless and barefoot, and he left damp tracks as he crossed the room to yank shut the draperies and close out the motel people, the parking lot, the elaborate shadow work of the giant palm tree.

He had mixed a drink for himself: four parts bourbon and one part tap water.

Now he leaned over the sinks at the dressing counter and took the drink. I saw his sinewy back arch as he fought to keep down the jolt.

He made it to the bed, where he dropped, looking stunned.

"So much for Doctor Jekyll," Raymond said. "Here comes Hyde."

"Jekyll put in a full day," I said.

Raf asked, "You been having fun with my wife, Raymond?"

"We been screwin' our brains out," Raymond said.

"That'd be a short session," said Raf.

"All we did was drive back here, hoss. To take you to supper with us."

Raf snorted, full of hate for the idea. "Food's a long way off," he said.

I signed us on for another week at the Park Inn.

"What's the story?" Raf said. "Why'd you re-up?"

"For *you*. I'm waiting for you," I said.

"The fuck. You just don't want to say goodbye to Raymond."

He slept away the day, coming awake like a vampire, at sundown.

Night, we drove over to The Yellow Man. The club seemed safe and friendly. A step-up platform stage had been added for live entertainment—a reggae band. And for dancing, a stretch of floor was spotlighted and cleared of tables.

Raf switched over to drinking sweetsie cocktails made with fruit syrups and cream. "See if maybe my skin'll quit crawling," he said.

The sugar-liquor combo animated him, but gave him manic rage. After three drinks he left me alone at our table and sauntered over to dance with some spare woman. I heard him threaten to thrash a man who knocked into them. And I had a feeling Raf wouldn't much mind *getting* thrashed.

At six or so, I swam in the Park Inn's lighted pool. The water was lukewarm. I pedaled on my back, stirring up a gleaming white wake, and watched dawn change the face of the sky. I saw morning birds.

There were no calls, no messages at the desk from Raymond.

Until noon, I lay taking sun on one of the webbed lounge chairs that crowded the patio. Noon brought the real factory heat.

Toward dark, I was waiting alone in the Firecat on a dead street in the Third Ward. Raf had gone inside one of these houses to see a doctor—"like a doctor," he had said, rather—about drying out.

"I'm sick of drinking," he had said.

"And sick *from* it," I had added.

"Don't help me, Paige, it hurts," he had said.

For something to do, I opened the glove compartment, and by its little light practiced writing quatrains. I made a kyrielle that became a pantoum because lines 2 and 4 of each stanza worked well as lines 1 and 3 of the next: A-B-A-B, B-C-B-C, C-D-C-D, and so on.

Raf materialized on the dark sidewalk, the handkerchief pocket of his black suit stuffed with papers, a printed pamphlet, a prescription sheet.

Back beside me in the car he said, "Did you go to high school, Paige?"

"Of course I did. You have to, don't you? It's a law."

"Never heard you talk about it."

"Well, I went," I said. "In Maryland and then we moved to Massachusetts. Why?"

"Close your eyes," he said, and his voice was soft, so I did.

"O.K., they're closed."

"I mean really tight. Squeeze them shut."

"There," I said, "done."

"Now, pretend you're back in high school."

"All right, I'm pretending. What happens next?"

"You lift your skirt and take down your panties."

"Oh no, Raf, uh unh. It can't be done. This is a compact car!"

"You're not pretending good, Paige."

"High school . . ." I said. "You're right. Yes it can."

"Nine and a half medium on these," Raf told a salesperson, and held up a pair of silver-trimmed running shoes. Collected on Raf's lap were some scanty shorts, socks, and a couple singlets.

We were in a sports clothes store—one in a line of shops in Rice Village.

"I'm not complaining about how expensive all this is," I said.

"Has to be," Raf said.

I said, "I hope you're not sobering up just to show me. I hope it's for yourself, or for, I don't know, not for nothing."

"Nothing's something," Raf said.

Raymond visited the motel that weekend and guessed in an instant that Raf had started drink withdrawal.

"'Anguish in my soul,'" Raymond said. "'How long, O Lord, how long?' That's Psalm six. Or it's thirteen, maybe. . . ."

Raf wore his running shorts. He was bent over, hands on knees, sweating still. He looked as though he'd been bucketed with water.

"Five motherfuckin' miles," he said.

"You ran five miles? Out there in that hell?"

"Limped through four of them. Swam laps here first, though."

"I guess you went crazy total," said Raymond. "It's sad to see."

"It's tragedy," Raf said. "You're watchin' it blithely."

He straightened up, tipped the motel's filled ice bucket to his face, and munched a mouthful of cubes. "I'm not here," he said, "just not here."

Raymond said, "You'll come back gradually. A part at a time, as I recall."

"I wish the part of me that sleeps'd come back. I bought a prescription from that quack Googie," Raf said. He showed Raymond a clear vial of white capsules.

"I hate that lizard Googie but it'd be dangerous going with nothin'. This is O.K. It's what they give you in the hospital," Raymond said.

"Fuck hospitals," said Raf.

"How 'bout vitamins? Are you eating?" Raymond asked.

"Some," Raf said. He lowered into a chair and peeled off a blood-streaked running sock. "Fruit juices. I'm working myself up for solid foods."

"Listen, you two," Raf said, hitching into a baggy pair of cargo jeans I'd brought along. He'd just finished showering.

Raymond took off his dark glasses as if to hear better. He crossed his arms, leaned a shoulder against the wall.

"I know what's going on between you. I could get it from looking at *Paige* when you're around, Raymond. And I also know how bad I messed up with Luisa. I'm sorry. But listen to me now. I'm going on a long stroll. You'd both be doing me a favor if you'd just get the fuck on with it."

"Wait, wait, Raf, please. Not one of your long strolls," I said.

"I'll be back," he said. "Before morning."

"You *think* you mean this," said Raymond. "You're coming out of a fog. There's self-recrimination . . ."

"Raymond, just do it or don't. Look, you know how *I* am, and it's gotta be the same for Paige. You can't tell me you don't want this, either of you, so have it," Raf said. And in seconds he yanked the door open on the fiery day and fled.

"Hope he meant that," Raymond said, unbuttoning his workshirt.

"Well, thank you, but . . ." I said.

"Sure *sounded* like he did," Raymond said. He kicked out of his boots. "Want me to undress you, peach?"

"Raymond, of course, I'd like to . . ." I said. "The idea's

been with me since the night we met. In fact, minus the idea, life'll be less something—a lot less."

He took my hand and we circled together and slow-danced.

I said, "And ordinarily I don't have such thoughts. My whole time with Raf I haven't, not about one other person."

"So what's in the way? My religion? What's to stop you?"

"You two," I said.

Raymond thought a moment and sighed. "Another day at the turkey facility," he said.

"Pardon?"

"Don't know, but it sums up how I feel."

Fists knotted, Raf paced a path in the motel carpeting—back and forth, back and forth. He ran. He whapped out laps in the pool. A couple or even three times a day he'd get me into bed for a full workout; or he climbed into the shower with me. Once he tackled me on an isolated little patch of lawn down around the vending machines.

We were on twenty-four-hour time: banking at a cash machine at 3 a.m.; buying fruit and groceries at sunup in Jacinto's.

He read anything. I brought him magazines, *Antaeus*, the *TLS*. At the Brazos Bookstore on Bissonnet I bought for him a slender novel from Brazil, the diary of a dead painter, a new play by an Irishwoman.

He wanted noise—the radio on. He listened to the jazz station, or the student broadcasts from Rice. He watched two-star movies on the TV's cable channels, watched whatever came on.

One night he left the news channel blaring on TV, and the newscasters' voices mingled with my dreams. As we rolled out of bed in the morning, I said, "Anything you want to know about Sissy Wallcock, the little liver baby, just ask me. I know what Sissy ate yesterday on her birthday. I know what presents she got, besides the new liver."

"Aw, I heard all that. I was awake," Raf said. "But then I harkened and changed over to *Route 66.*"

"You did? Which episode?" I asked.

"Todd poses as an American Nazi and to prove his loyalty to the group he has to beat up Buz."

"That's a good one," I said.

He slept now as I gazed through the motel window at all the car metal glimmering in the lot below, in the beam of a full moon.

I drifted down to the Firecat and crawled inside. I pretended my parents, Mario and Dottie, were young again, still married, riding on either side of me. I pretended they were la-la-la-ing along with the radio as it played Scarlatti—quick-music/slow-music/quick-music; an Italian overture, the origin of symphony.

Mono Astro, a hair place, hadn't been able to schedule me in until our last day at the Park Inn.

Raf asked, "Are you getting it all whacked off, Paige?"

"I have to see, I haven't decided."

"Just get it whacked off. Let's both do, in fact," he said. "I'm coming along."

Mono Astro had an Asian theme inside. There were empty areas and blank walls, paper screens, neutral colors.

Raf dropped into a long chair that folded out in sections. He whistled along with the music surrounding us—a song by Turnpike People.

I told the woman who seemed to be running things that I wanted a shampoo, a cut, maybe a cellophane rinse.

"Maybe yes or maybe no?" she asked. Her natural voice was a whisper. Weedy sprouts of hair stood up on her scalp.

"I'm not sure yet," I said.

"I want Vampira there to work on me," Raf said.

"He likes you," I explained.

"I'm married," the woman whispered.

She introduced a man who resembled her, who had the same traumatized hair. This was Boomer, her husband.

I got horizontal in the deeply padded chair with my neck arched, my head tipped back, my hair flung in a sink.

Boomer kept quiet as he shampooed me, gathering my hair in great sopping snatches and making lathery spears with it. I closed my eyes and listened to the crackle of foam bubbles. He massaged my scalp, my temples; lulled me into drowsiness.

Raf wasn't lulled. He chattered at the whispering woman, whom he called Barber-ah, and he wouldn't let go of the tiny joke.

"You think I should get an earring, Barber-ah?"

"Wouldn't know. Ask your wife."

"You do pierce jobs, don't you? Or am I too old for an earring?"

"Your wife might know," the woman said.

Raf said, "Boomer, give my wife a back-to-school cut, O.K.? I'll buy her a lunch pail and a little matching knapsack."

"My students probably don't want to be taught by someone who looks like their little brother," I said.

"I hate doing kids," said the whispering woman. "More than anything. You're a teacher?"

"I'm on leave this year," I said.

Raf said, "Do you ever take a leave, Barber-ah? Do a vacation?"

"I'm Lois. No. Hold still."

"Aw, are we cranky? Do we need a sip of blood to feel better?" Raf said.

Behind me, Boomer sighed mightily.

"I know," I said to him.

"You don't shave, do you?" Raf asked Lois.

"No, we don't do shaves. Not in this salon. It isn't permitted to smoke in here, sir."

"I know it," Raf said. "I just want to make you angry so you give me a mean haircut, not a Houston haircut. You're not from Houston, I hope."

"I'm a native."

"Tell you what I think of Houston . . ."

"Raf!" I said.

"I adore it," he said.

"We're happy to hear it. All Houstonians are relieved about that," Lois said.

"I meant *you* don't shave. Under your arms. I see up your sleeves you don't."

"Is he really named Raft or did he make it up?" Boomer asked me.

"Does it bother you, sir?" Lois was saying to Raf.

"Does Boomer want his butt pumped?" Raf said.

Lois balled up her hand towel and threw it. "I don't have to take this," she said.

"Then I don't have to pay any forty fuckin' dollars," said Raf. He was standing now, with the body-length bib still tied around his neck, smoking and flicking ashes at Lois.

"Laws," she said to him. "One phone call."

It was a hundred and five degrees outside the salon. As we rushed for the car and its air conditioning, I said, "I don't think you were being fair in there."

"Nothing is no goddamned fair, Paige. You should've fucked Raymond."

"And another thing," he said as he was driving. "I don't approve of us. Where are we going next, for example—the fuckin' dry cleaners! Maybe afterwards we could do budget."

He sped up, pressing pedal to the floor on a road called the Buffalo Speedway.

YELLOW NOTE,
BLUE NOTE

THE CAR was idling in the Park Inn's loading zone.

Raf hurled our bags into the trunk and whomped shut the door with full force.

I yelled, "I can't put up with you like this, Raf! Your great big emotions! *No more.*"

"You have to go in with me," he said, driving onto the sandlot for a used-car dealership in the Fifth Ward.

"Why, are we buying a car?"

We were. An '81 Seeger-Z hatchback automatic the color of smoke, we were buying. With tax it cost five hundred dollars.

Our salesman was heat frantic in the glass-walled office. In metal-tipped boots, he clomped back and forth; fists balled up in the pockets of his vanilla suit pants. He had the phone receiver caught between his shoulder and ear. We sat waiting in scoop chairs. He arranged for a title, registration, plates.

"This is a good car we're buying?" I asked Raf.

"Umm, no."

"But it'll run?"

"For a month at least."

"Why are we buying such a car?"

"Consider the rental rates and gas for that thunder mobile you got," he said. "This's a money move. Same reason we're renting a house."

"Where? What city?"

"This city. I spotted it yesterday, doing my five miles. I already talked to the landlady. We're buying a car, renting a house. . . . We'll be set for what's to come."

"*Leaving* is to come! Why aren't we leaving?"

"Paige," Raf said. "Apart from your being in love with Raymond . . . We haven't served out our sentences yet."

Raf's choice of house was a tilting two-story whose wood siding needed paint. Before the house and its garage lay a yellow patch of yard with a three-foot Francis of Assisi birdbath.

A boat on a trailer took up the driveway.

"Boat," I said. Its hull and cabin were salt-eaten, both the same noncolor as the house.

"That's no pleasure craft," Raf told me. "That mother worked for a living."

He led me onto the house porch, where a few old metal folding chairs were gathered.

I saw across the street a low cinderblock structure—the Stonewall Jackson Elementary. Neighboring to the south was a brick apartment building. A paper sign on its padlocked entry door said, DESGLAISES MENTAL HEALTH HOSPITAL—CLOSED FOR REPAIRS. Through fronds and elephant grass off the other porch rail, I made out the furrowed wall of a liquid-oxygen company.

"Houston has no zoning laws," Raf said.

He said, "The house is unlocked. You can go on in."

"But do I want to?" I said. "Raf, really. You've got summer-school kids across the street, yowling because they're hot and miserable and have to go to summer school; a condemned mental asylum next door; an explosives factory in the side yard . . ."

"My kind of place," Raf said.

"And now we're driving a car that some boys built in metal shop. I truly dislike you."

"Well," he said, "I know."

We got my bags and Raf's bundles of running gear inside.

The living room was narrow and dark, and although the windows were propped open, warm.

"No air conditioning," I said.

"One hundred a month, furnished, utilities paid. Be realistic, Paige. What can you expect?"

I stalked into the kitchen. It was better. Through the rear windows, a thicket of weeds and wild flowers gave off sweet smells. I heard a cricket, and birds.

I went back to the living room. Raf had taken off his shirt. He lay on a blue vinyl sofa he'd dragged into a breeze from the screen door.

His face looked suffered, sharpened. "Come over here and kneel down," he said.

"No you don't. I need to talk to you about bugs."

"*El remedio es* Black Flag."

"What about rats, then, and lizards?"

"Plenty of both. Come on, Paige." His hand moved to unsnap his Levi's.

I rummaged in my satchel and threw the first thing I

found—a five-pound anthology of Deep Image poetry. I missed him with that, but flung a ceramic mug and connected just over his eyebrow. He caught the mug on the rebound and held it protectively. I slung my notebook at him, a bottle of nail lacquer, my pocket calculator, sunglasses, a packet of tampons, triple-A batteries.

"You tick, Raf," I said. "You lowlife."

He didn't raise an arm or duck but permitted the storm as if it were his due.

"You don't want to live here?" he asked finally.

"Live!" I said. "I don't want to *know* about here."

Raf rode me around the new neighborhood to show me its sidewalk charms. We saw an Asian couple pushing a grocery carriage full of aluminum soda cans, some kids trapping a dog in a hammock.

A rooster picked its way across the street ahead of us. Raf pumped the brake pedal and we slam-stopped.

"Look at that moron," Raf said.

The rooster twisted his head to glare at us. His eye was like a chip of some glossy stone—a mineral eye.

"I think you were going too fast," I said.

Raf shook his head no. He was smiling. He said, "Come on, you gotta like the fuckin' bird."

Raf was as happy as he ever got, in the Desglaises Street house. The furniture was indestructible, so he could tumble it, climb on it, kick and send the castered chairs rolling.

He mounted a unit air conditioner in our bedroom window, and the machine kept the whole upstairs meat-locker cold.

"Say what you will, there is no television here," he said.

"And there will *be* no fuckin' television. And no telephone either."

The place was like a 1930s gangsters' hole-up, but the days, I found, did have more time in them.

Early in the afternoon, the summer-school kids crowded the walk at the end of our yard. Raf and I sat on the porch together, on the metal folding chairs, and watched students board a long navy-blue school bus.

"Look at the one in the camouflage outfit. They have ROTC for elementary grades now?" Raf said.

I said, "There are soldiers in Africa who are not that old."

"I think there should be more fat kids," he said. "I count only two. If I had a fuckin' kid, I'd make sure he was fat. Or she. You can't love 'em otherwise."

"You want to bounce them around."

"Fat as buddhas," Raf said.

I rented a Toro from the corner hardware and mowed the yellow lawn along a trail of shade cast by the liquid-oxygen company. I raked and bagged the grass clippings; edged with a new pair of shears.

This yellow grass was sweet, sodded to an anatomy of slopes and ridges that were gentle as a boy's back.

"It's like carpet," Raymond said from the porch.

When I finished, I joined him there and drank a frothy Tecate.

Raymond tossed a silver coin into the yard. He said, "There you go, see? It's long enough to lose a dime but short enough that you could find it, you know where to look."

"I've never heard that," I said.

"Well, it's the right length for July."

Raymond was different around me—acting shy as a shadow.

"After Princeton," Raymond said now. "After they cut me loose, naturally I lost my student deferment."

"Couple years before I did," Raf said, dropping onto a chair between us.

"Ummm," I said.

"Some story," said Raymond.

I said, "Everyone who was around back then has a story, and there isn't one that I want to hear."

"A deal we have," Raf explained to Raymond.

"I busted out," Raymond said. "Not as honorably as they'd of liked."

"Me too. Me neither," Raf said.

"You guys," I said. "Do you mind? Raf, you promised you wouldn't."

The dance club we frequented now was the Palm, and here Raf seemed driven by some decisive engine.

He paused at our table only long enough to gulp an iced coffee.

I said, "We are going home sometime—back East—right?"

"Guess so," he said and shrugged.

"Because if you're never going back you ought to tell me, Raf. I always thought we were happy in Brookline. . . ."

He stopped me with a dark look.

"A functional phrase, 'we were happy,' " I said. "Apart

from a few obvious things: That it's cold. Students, and they call too often. You're not allowed to park your car anywhere . . ."

He was leaving even as I recited.

I watched him move toward a woman in a knitted bubble of mini skirt; watched as he asked her to dance.

"And you have to tiptoe up and down the fire escape," I continued, "every time you want to sneak Christy away from her husband. Anna doesn't *have* a fire escape so if Juan comes home you've gotta jump from the balcony. Sometimes when Daphne phones for you I answer. . . ."

The hotel where my father and I stayed in Cameroon was called the Pilot. It stood to the side of a runway for a dead airport. The runway had a pink stucco radar tower, blind, its windows smashed to crystal.

There were customs sheds in use as caravansaries, and piled around were blackened bales of wool.

We could hear sheep bleating. Sometimes they'd cough like humans.

We could see Mount Cameroon from the windows. At night, tribesmen would set the brush on the mountain's top afire.

We could see a dust field with a shrunken tree. Heat, we saw. No signs. No billboards.

The Pilot had a sandstone saloon that was noisy all the time from music and fights.

One evening, salesmen from Duaka visited. These were men with pale shoes that matched their pale suits. They met with women in dresses and took photographs of them with an Instamatic camera—flash bombs of light that made us blink.

I went upstairs early that night, climbed the three flights

to my bedroom above. I sat in a square armchair. The radio had picked up a thirsty gargling. Pinned on the walls here were sepia-toned illustrations, carefully torn from a children's Christmas book.

I brushed palm oil into my hair—brittle from the sun. I was twitchy; thinking, "Lonesome" and "Bored," and about Raf.

He was in love that summer with someone. Mario knew this and took me away.

If there was any sense in teaching, it was for someone such as Millicent, in one of my first Harvard workshops.

She once situated herself in the Commons Room at Adams House for ten hours, writing hymnal measure, quantitative and syllabic verse.

I heard that her friends suggested she move along, to her quarters or to the cafeteria; heard that she swore at them.

From the one working phone booth outside the Fiesta I called South Houston State and asked to speak to Davey Salizar. I'd known Davey since graduate school. He was director this August, of the SHS Adult Education Conference.

"Is there any kind of opening for me?" I asked. "What do you have left?"

In fact, there was a slot teaching poetry writing to physicists. Davey said that some program advisor in administration had the idea of cross-discipline courses, and that dozens of scientists were enrolling for month-long classes on music theory, drama, film technique, dance history, glass blowing, and writing verse.

I found Raf checking expiration dates on orange-juice cartons in the Fiesta's dairy section.

I said, "I might do some teaching while I'm here."

"Sure, sure, and Little Sheba will come home, and the three sisters will leave the Cherry Orchard finally and go to Moscow, and a gentleman will come calling for Blanche."

"No, not a real department job," I said, as he loaded tubs of yogurt and cakes of tofu into the shopping cart. "Just August at SHS. They have a summer arts festival."

"You haven't got a month's teaching left in you, Paige. Ten years of it and you're like a hunted thing around students."

"I've thought this."

"It's bad for you," he said. "It is bad. It's the worst."

The office lent to me at SHS had gray walls, charts, window shades, heavy black oak furniture, shelves of hardbacks.

August was at full fry. Cicadas sizzled all over everywhere. These were thumb-sized cicadas with sectioned powdery-black torsos. They looked like Inuit soapstone carvings with tomato-red beads for eyes, gold-lacquered wings.

When Raf phoned, I said, "Their noise sounds calculated, like song compositions. I have one going in my head right now that I don't want to lose. 'Bug-bug-bug.' It's a yellow note followed by a blue note."

"You fucked any of the physicists yet?" Raf asked.

"They're weird but not my kind of weird," I said.

Barny I was thinking, for example. He had a beard and he'd been around Stanford in the quark search days. He had no skill for poetry but as a particle physicist he reported, "We think we have the answers to just about everything."

"Can you imagine even *thinking* that?" I asked Raf.

From Freedom Hall, where class gathered, we had an easterly view of the central quad with its statues of Sam Houston and Jefferson Davis and one in black rock of the school's mascot, a pug-faced Disneyish dinosaur.

I made my opening remarks: "Don't stick to these patterns and forms exactly. Just allude to them and don't worry about metricality or rhyming. The form'll be back there, influencing you, is all. Think more about musicality, although nobody give me song lyrics."

I said, "There isn't anything inherently great about rhyme or meter. They're just framing devices. But you can use them to control how we read the poem."

I went on talking until I ran out. I took roll. One older man there was someone whose submission I'd rejected. "Carl?" I said. "You're not ah, listed on my roster."

Carl was chewing gum. He said, "No bearing on the quality of your rejection, ma'am. The competition was considerable. I regret I'm unable to accept. I'm here."

The third class meeting, Dr. Gil from West Virginia said, "Here's a confession. I wrote a new program for my p.c. *It* wrote both efforts you've seen from me. I haven't contributed one verb, one article."

Dr. Gil's colleagues very much liked this confession. There was delighted supportive applause.

"Your poems, though—well, I mean, not yours but these—they're much better than other machined works I've seen," I said.

"Sure, I'm a computer scientist," Dr. Gil said. "Mine was an amazing program."

Raf would talk with me or go dancing in the evenings, but dawns, before I awoke, he'd be off running through the Fifth Ward.

From my borrowed office, over the phone I told him, "The cicadas sound more Cuban for some reason. Now I've got Cuban 'Bug-bug-bug.' "

My thoughts on him were like thin clear fish swirling through oil; they were polluted, slippery, transfixing.

"For tomorrow, I'd like you to choose one small thing to talk about that deals with prosody," I said. "And I want you to write a canzone. Seventeen lines with the syllables occurring in six stanzas and repeated in the same order. They're from French troubadours. Or you could try a provençal. They're unrhymed, and in praise of love or beauty."

I liked to have Barny in during office hours to talk about quark confinement.

"Tell me the flavors again," I said.

" 'Up' and 'Down' " Barny said, "were two of the first. And 'Strange.' Then 'Charm,' and next came 'Beautiful.' Last one was 'True.' "

I read aloud to the class a homework poem by Dr. Mali. I said, "Huh. Notice the one foot that isn't metrical. That's a terminal trochee. It calls attention to itself, so it's typically used for satire. Although not here."

————

During a meeting with Dr. Gil, I said, "Well, Dr. Gil. I think—don't you?—enough of your machine's poems. You fed it some Wallace Stevens, didn't you."

"Among others," he said.

There was a cicada corpse on my desk.

Across from me, Dr. Gil had the big chair with the revolving anatomy. Anyone who sat in this chair spun musingly left and right.

"Interestingly," he said, "that particular poem will be published in the *Little Summer* magazine. The editor over there, Debbie, tells me she finds it free of debris."

"That's because Debbie mostly sees poems about kittens or sunrises or sometimes there's a poem on how energetic the poet's grandparent is."

"Those're all good things," said Dr. Gil.

"Inarguably. But topics that have been addressed, you see."

"My grandmother is a hundred and eight years old," he said. "She deserves a poem."

"She deserves a great poem, by you."

"O.K., O.K.," Dr. Gil said. "If I'm permitted to write about Grandmother, to blazes with the computer. May I tell you a little about her life in the West Virginia Gorge?"

"Rhyme and meter are lulling, anesthetizing," I said to the class. "Their uses, for hypnotic effect, are antediluvian."

Barny said, "Well hell, professor."

"Paige."

"Professor Paige," he said. "I always thought scientists were more poetic than other people, in the Aristotelian sense. But in truth, as poets, we're weenies. I won't be coming to class anymore."

Wynton, a big-bellied man, agreed. "I'm baffled. I was willing to give it a try and I have, but enough," Wynton said.

"It seems such a wispy endeavor," said Harry, a young man from Oregon. Harry's head was terribly large.

"Count me out as well," Dr. Mali said. "At first I found poetry an exquisite puzzle, fully distracting to me. It involved a pleasant stress—avoiding sentiment, using finesse—trying to say what would seem unsayable. Now each night I dread the half hour at my word processor."

"But if you're all quitting, I'm out of a goddamn job!" I said. "People, please reconsider."

"That's the way it goes," someone said, and several of the class members shrugged.

I flumped into my chair seat, causing my briefcase to tip over. It disgorged papers, reference texts, index cards. I let them spill.

Harry said, "Paige, since this is our last meeting together, why don't you tell us a story."

I gave them some of the Gilgamesh epic. I told how Gilgamesh, king of Uruk, had a second self created by the gods and this being was a man called Enkidu.

"Enki Denki Doo," Carl said.

"This is an *old* story," Wynton said.

"It's third millennium," I said. "B.C., Archaic Sumerian . . ."

"Tell me, Paige. How am I different from the women you teach at Harvard?" asked Dr. Mali.

"They're all named Elizabeth," I said.

"My grandmother's name," said Dr. Gil.

———

Our bedroom in the rental house had soft warped wooden floors with runnels and gouges. On the plaster walls, cracks traced the shapes of states, continents.

I was in bed under a sheet, propped up with a pillow against the carved headboard. The carving was an Italian farm-life scene—animals and men, haymows, a wheelbarrow.

My heart banged.

The dream I'd just had said there was no death, that nothing was terminable. Everything kept existing in a big all and all.

Rain lashed the window now. Traffic on the wet street made surf sounds.

I watched the ceiling, which Raf had swabbed with marigold paint.

Something drew me from the bed to the window. A fellow stood in the yellow side yard beside the liquid-oxygen company. His breath was like steam. The summer rain weighted his old suit and bubbled on his face and hands and the lenses of his eyeglasses. He was any age, bald, still as a table lamp.

I needed a drink of water but I waited for the figure to move. A shrug or nod or a head twitch would've satisfied me, as long as the man did not dissolve.

It was always the walk-ons who gave me the shivers— the woman at the end of the subway platform; the boy planted at the exit door I had to get through; the lady asleep or dead on the restroom floor.

The man in the yard moved.

I stumbled to the stairs wanting water. Raf sat at the base, lacing up his shoes for his morning run. I told him about the dream. My heart was still whamming.

"Damn it, *I* need one of those," he said.

"Just a synaptical shortout probably, like a hiccup or a

muscle spasm. But in it I had memory, every thought I've ever had. . . . Do I look any different to you?"

"Only because of the pentagram on your forehead," Raf said.

For the rest of the day the dream lingered with me.

That evening, on the porch, Raf told me there are five billion people on the planet—about eighty-six for each square mile.

Dusk and rain had turned everything olive green and shiny.

I said writing poetry would be impossible, knowing such statistics.

"Or the other way: why *not* write?" he said.

I thought for a minute. "The turkey facility," I said.

He nodded.

"What happened to Raymond?" I asked. "He's been by only once."

"Haven't talked to him. You want me to?"

"Sure," I said.

"Why?"

"Why *not*?"

"You're suggesting we should see other people?"

I said, "Raf, sometimes your mentality's straight from *Teen Beat*. This morning I see God, tonight I'm in some sock-hop situation."

"That is the variety of the life experience," he said.

From here I could see into the strange house, into the dining room, where there were four chairs now, and a round-topped table, a corner cupboard with a stack of brown-patterned plates, a pewter coffee service Raf had bought secondhand. There were floor lamps flanking the table, their bulbs burning gold under manila paper shades.

"I'll call Raymond," he said. He gazed off at the boat docked in our driveway.

Raymond had his wicker chair tipped on its hind legs; his boots resting on a vacant seat. With a bone-handled knife he was skinning a green apple. He said, "At Princeton, everybody took Raf's low moods serious 'cause he was a philosophy major. So if you were havin' a good day and you forgot all about your ontological center, he could make you feel like a bunny-fucking moron."

The restaurant was sunny, done in whites and reds. Paco's Cantina, it was called.

"Spreads joy, don't he," Raymond said.

"Like a stain," I said.

Raymond wore a frayed denim shirt and, against the room's brightness, his dark glasses.

I said, "It's why he left Oxford, why he never finished his dissertation. He thinks recorded philosophy has no value because the act of composing a text or an essay or tractus means the philosopher wasn't deranged and despairing enough."

"Whoa, big catch-twenty-two," Raymond said.

Of the apple peel he was making an unbroken coil, a perfect spiral.

"Are you going to eat that when you're finished?" I asked.

"Well, no," Raymond said, and looked as though perhaps he should apologize. He said, "Raf stopped laying any of that on me. Must've seen how it was spoiling my program. He knows better 'n to bring it up."

"Still does with me," I said.

"You two are weird," Raymond said. "Though I wish you both well. I honestly do."

Our waiter delivered our lunch orders—chimichangas and spiced corn.

"You want this necklace, *amigo?*" Raymond asked the waiter. "Give it to your girl?" He was offering the coil of apple peel.

All afternoon we rode around in Raymond's green convertible. He showed me the downtown—Louisiana Street, the Interfirst Bank Building, which Hurricane Alicia had smashed into; a Dubuffet sculpture titled "Monument to The Phantom" in the plaza; on Milan, the Tex Comm Tower with its Miró sculpture, a steel work called "Personage with Birds."

We angled on one-way streets—past Tranquility Park, built for the first moon landing; past Sam Houston Park, where, Raymond said, there used to be a zoo.

He said, "Oil wasn't *all*, don't think that. We're still the leader on mineral products. Sulfur, helium, graphite, other stuff, clay . . . There's plenty to do, and deserted mansions you can rent. I don't know why Raf's got you living over in the Mother Teresa district.

"Look at that palm. That's a Coco Plumoso. I wanted to name our daughter Coco Plumoso but Luisa said no. See the dead part on top, looks like the skirt on a hula girl? There's rats in there. You got a queen palm, you better keep it trimmed back or you get rats."

We drove the Southwest Freeway and veered off to ride alongside the Brazos River. Raymond said, "Oldest story's that it was named Brazos de Dios—Arms of God—by Coronado. Him and his men was about to die of thirst when some of our Indians guided 'em to water."

"What kind of Indians?" I asked.

"Ah, they'd have been Comanch, mainly," he said. "And littler tribes too, like the Tawakoni. But Chickasaw, Apache, Cherokee. You name it, they was here, and I mean *here* here."

Raf once told me that at the zoo where he worked as a teenager, when rainstorms broke, the big cats would copulate—the leopards, the lions. I asked him, "Really?" And he said, "Well, it's what I remember," as if his remembering were enough.

He was seated at the round-top dining table over a copy of *The Schopenhauer Reader*. Its jacket was cracked and curled.

"Well, what happened?" he asked me. "How'd it go? Why didn't Raymond come in?"

"He went to take Luisa and the baby to the pediatric clinic. Nothing happened."

"What all'd you talk about?"

"Not anything in particular," I said. "You know. A lot of stuff. And we rode around."

The light was spooky, coming through the window as if aiming at Raf; contained around him, and not spread over the depths of the dark room.

He said, "You don't really need me anymore, do you, Paige?"

"It's what I remember," I said.

Raf's look now was piercing. He said, "You mean you have just a kind of shadow need for me."

"No no," I said. "Never mind."

"You troll," I said to Schopenhauer.

———

A blonde and her brunette sister had their punched-in pickup behind the boat in our drive. A sign, stickered to the driver's door, read: WE NEED BILINGUAL HELP—CALL 629-7071.

I led the two women inside.

They were neighbors from a block down and they were including me in their weekly card game.

"Del will be coming," the blonde said.

The brunette was an overstuffed woman with a careworn face, deep wrinkles, bristling hair glinting with gray.

The blonde wore black shorts and a black tank top. She looked young enough to be the brunette's child.

They got seated at the table. The blonde riffled a deck of Bicycle-brand playing cards.

The brunette splashed coins onto the table, shoved them into roughly sorted piles. She put out a few dollar bills as well.

"Watch that and make sure she don't steal it," she told each of us about the other.

She wandered out to the truck and brought back Mexican beer, which she pushed into the refrigerator. She served us uncapped bottles and popped open a cellophane bag of peanuts.

"Those salted in the shell?" the blonde asked.

We shucked shells and ate peanuts. I drank my beer from the bottle and scratched at its label just as they were doing.

"That's right," the blonde said, eyeing me. "You get that off in one straight tear, it means you're a virgin."

"Goddamn Del," said the brunette. "She ruins every game."

"Just late," the blonde said. "She's always late. Resign yourself."

An ice-cream truck with a tinkling bell was swerving around in the street.

The brunette said, "I always pictured a Harvard teach with a tight hair bun and a shawl."

"Yeah, a shawl she knitted herself, 'cause that's her entertainment," the blonde said.

"If you want to think that," I said. "It's still America."

"Ain't it just," the brunette said.

A redhead arrived—Del. She was thick-haunched and slow-walking. She wore a housedress and had five glass-stone rings on her left hand.

"In a dress yet," the brunette said.

"I gotta work," the redhead said. "You all can go around in your bathing suits, that's fine. But I'm a working girl."

The redhead's job, the sisters explained, was as entry guard at the Magnolia City dump.

"What she calls a 'landfill project,' " the brunette said.

"Could I have a bigger chair please?" the redhead asked me. "Chrissakes," I heard her whisper.

"Yeah, Paige," the blonde said. "Drag in your sofa for Del's bottom."

After we'd played four hands, the brunette said, "I'm about wiped out. I got twenty-five, forty, a dollar. A dollar and a dime."

The redhead—whose game was furious, with no wasted moves and a sense of time running out—told the blonde, "Lend your sister twenty."

"Right, I'll do that, sweet thing," the blonde said. "The same day I eat tin."

"Deal," she said to me.

"Come on, come on," said the redhead.

"I quit anyway, with this hand," the brunette said. "With

what I got dealt?" She fanned her cards. "Forget about it."

"Anybody? Or is this my pot already?" asked the redhead. She scraped up the bills. She scooped change into her ringed hands and in four trips plunged it all into the patch pockets of her housedress. "Well, ladies," she said to us.

"Look at her gloat. Can you stand it?" the brunette asked.

"I can stand it," said the blonde.

"You lose your three dollars?" the brunette said. "Our hearts bleed. I lost grocery money."

"Listen to her whining. Who stole the violins?" said the redhead.

Across the road, kids erupted from the elementary school and a few dogs arrived to bark the children aboard their navy-blue bus.

The blonde said, "So, potatoes. Where you goin' next?"

"Call me potatoes, sure," the redhead said. "But I jingle when I walk, lady, and it's your dough. What do I owe for the beer?" she asked.

"Hundred and ten dollars," said the blonde.

"A thousand dollars," the brunette said.

The redhead dabbed her thumb on her tongue and wiped two bills from the stash in her pocket. "Schlitz beer was it?"

When she was gone, the blonde said, "God, I hate Del. I hate men more, though. Any and all men, including Robert."

"Then you're pig stupid," the brunette said.

"No, it's that I'm sick of pricks," said the blonde. "Especially the men nowadays. Blah."

"You lez," the brunette said.

"You tell me, then. What are they after? First they hit

you, then they cry. They got me in more trouble in my life and kept me more broke than everything else all put together."

"They've messed me up," I said, and surprised myself a little. I squinted at my Mazatlán beer.

The brunette, shuffling cards, nodded and shook her head alternately. Now and then she peered over at me, measuring whether or not I was serious. Finally she said, "I *guess* it's true for me too." Her lined face was all concern, though. She said, "But I still *like* my old man."

"Flippo, we all like Andy," said the blonde. "Andy's one of the good ones, not who we're criticizing. Though I bet even he has his moods."

"Oh, he'll hit me in the eye," the brunette said.

"The time?" Raf asked me.

"Um, central, subtract an hour, it's nearly five."

"O.K., come on. A performance thing to show you," he said. "Although walking into this abstemious will be weird."

He drove us to an upscale community where on either side of a four-lane highway ran a mile of mall and villages of condos. Everything around was elaborately planted. There were vines and snaking ropes of ivy.

The mall offered a boxcar line of retail stores—Roy's Jewelers, Ann Taylor, Video Rentals and Sales, Pattie Pauley's Academy of Dance. We parked midway, before an unmarked building painted steel blue.

"Is this gonna be more lowlife, Raphael?"

"Well, yes. Or no. You'll see."

Now I noticed the establishment's framed poster. It was unillustrated, with simple printing: SWEETNESS—ADULT ENTERTAINMENT.

"I can't go in there," I said.

"You can, in fact. In fact, this's a white-collar couples' place."

"What does *that* mean?"

"It means men and women go in."

A fellow who looked like banking or middle management—young, cautious—approved our clothes and said, "Welcome, take any table. Waitress'll be with you."

Behind us, the slow-swinging door shut and we were caught in a dark aisle. Raf guided me to a table on a stairstep row.

The table had a linen drape, a generous ashtray, a lamp with a small shade. Tethered to the chairs were silver helium balloons.

Pink and white paper streamers dangled from the ceiling. Mirrors hung wherever a mirror would fit.

A disk jockey was babbling into a microphone from a Vegas-style stage. On a runway that jutted from the stage posed a girl in white boots and a G-string with loopy elastic suspenders.

Big heavily amped music pounded.

"See?" Raf said. "Lots of couples here."

There were couples seated at the various tables, men and women wearing business suits.

"Raf!" I said. "That dancer just waved at you."

"I know her slightly. Her name's Pru."

Pru did a handstand, and while upside down, stamped her white boots on the mirror behind.

"How about *that*?" asked the d.j.

Pru scissored out of the handstand. She cartwheeled, landed in a gymnast's leg split with her bottom flush to the floor.

"Yipes," I said.

"She claims you gotta do stuff like that these days," Raf said.

"Is it sexy?" I asked him. "I honestly would like to know."

"Yeah, Paige, it's considered sexy."

We ordered Cokes. "That's four-fifty for each," the waitress said.

I said, "No, can't be right."

"We understand," Raf told her.

"I know you. Hey," the pretty waitress said, bending low to study Raf.

All the waitresses were pretty; more like beauty-pageant contestants than drink slingers in a stripper place.

"Your hair may be different but I know I remember you."

"Never been here," Raf said.

"Yeah, you have. Remember? There was a fight or something?"

"Look, I've never been here." he said. "And direct Pru over to us as soon as she finishes."

A deeply drunk man wandered from his table to the stage.

Pru sidled up to the drunk and, with her white boots far apart, did a rotational hip grind.

The drunk man beamed.

"He loves it!" said the d.j. "Show her some green for her trouble."

Pru knelt and let the drunk customer drop folded bills down into the slingshot V of her G-string. She bounded up and resumed her dance.

"Does she have to do that part?"

"Incessantly," said Raf.

He glanced around annoyed. He said, "You see how

embarrassing this place is. You don't wanna look but there's Pru doin' double backflips, yet you know she's so bored she's counting the seconds. So if you look, you're a fool, but ignoring her's insulting, especially when she's a friend."

"How many friends do you have here, Raf?"

"Only Pru. We came to pick her up one night and there were, you know, assorted wretchednesses ensuing."

"A fight?"

"Not much of one," Raf said. The iris of his glass eye picked up some of the red-pink lighting. "Mostly bad talk. All mine. You can imagine."

"You want food?" he asked me. "They got chips, I'm sure, or they could Xerox a sandwich."

"Pass, but thanks anyway," I said.

In the mist of colored spots, Pru seemed unreal, more hologram than live woman. She looked tactile and dimensional, but at the same time a projected image.

I said, "I'll grant this. She's perfect."

Pru twisted into a complicated painful-looking position. On her neck, the pressure of the pose made a vein bulge the size of my little finger.

A group of men whooped.

" 'The lust of the goat is the bounty of God. The wrath of the lion is the . . . something . . . of God,' " Raf said.

I helped him. " 'The wisdom.' "

"Right, and " 'The nakedness of woman is the work of God.' "

"But Blake never spent time in the locker rooms at the Y," I said.

As Pru finished her act on her belly, she seemed passionately involved with the surface of the stage.

She left and was replaced by a garbed woman, soon to be ungarbed.

I had drunk my cola and risked teeth by chewing the remaining ice cubes.

Pru emerged from a dressing room. She strolled to our table; nodded hello to Raf, smiled bashfully at me. She wore mules and a dragon-lady dress, weed green.

"Never figured I'd see you back here," she told Raf.

"My wife, Paige," he said.

"No fuckin' way. Really? You know I've read all the poems in that one collection of yours or the—what do you call it?—chapbook. 'At the Clam Bar' or something—that one."

"And I've seen you dance," I said.

"No, I mean, why would you believe me, but I love your poems. I probably sound asinine. And that wasn't dancing, that was just my *job*," said Pru.

"I don't think you need apologize to Paige," Raf said.

"I was impressed by how well you did your job," I said.

Pru said, "You wouldn't guess, but this is a highly competitive field. Girls have to audition hard to dance here. But then they make fuckin' bundles, and it's clean work —no side stuff unless they want. But you do have to perform in some way—have a special thing, you know? It's why I do the contortionist shit. See Tanya? She almost made the Olympics when she was young but she got too tall."

"Paige is new in town," Raf said.

"How do you like it?" asked Pru.

The doorman in the banker's grays had moved close to us.

"He wants me to hustle drinks," Pru said.

"I like it fine," I said.

Pru stared at me.

Raf lit a cigarette to cut into the silence.

"Excuse me, you *like* Houston?" Pru said.

"Ah, sure."

"You got that one poem, I forgot the title, but it's about Mercury as the morning star and how all the sidewalks smell like bad meat?"

"Something like that," I said. "Not my cheeriest work."

"I *live* by it," Pru said.

"It kept me indoors for a while," Raf said.

"I'm just so astounded you like Houston. I mean, you wanna know why I work here? You probably don't care."

"Well, I do wonder, in fact. You don't have to say, but feminism aside . . ."

"Contempt," Pru said.

"Now you're talking," said Raf.

"Yeah, 'cause it's too late in history for feminism to make any difference, Paige. It's all coming down. I'm only alive for contempt."

"What's coming down?" I asked. "You sound as though you've been enrolled in Raf's joy-of-living seminar."

"Everything. Every goddamn thing's coming down. Look at who's president! Or back up to the Iowa primary and who won that—a fuckin' televangelist! When Pat Robertson can get enough votes to be in charge of roach removal, then I'm living in the wrong damn country. I especially despise the South," Pru said. She looked left and right—a spy-movie gesture as if checking for listeners. "I mean to rub my bare *ass* in the South's face."

I said, "The thing is, I don't imagine the South minds your doing that too much."

"You could pretend *I'm* the South," Raf said.

Pru said, "I hate every pinhead in a ballcap, who drives a pickup truck, shoots deer, kisses my tits on Saturday, the Bible on Sunday. . . ."

"Wait, wait, hold it. Then why do you live here?" I asked her.

"I won't for long. I'm getting out. Me, my daughter, we're migrating to Canada. Fleeing before the Inquisition, if there's time."

Raf had shut his eyes and smiled along with Pru's attack as if she were thumping a drum solo.

"I hate the U.S. I hate the South. I hate men," she listed.

"Oh me, more of that," I said.

"So I work as a stripper and gorge on contempt. I'm like on *fire* with it. It keeps me fueled," Pru said.

"You really hate men?"

"And women," Pru said. "Although not you."

"Raf?" I asked.

"He's O.K. *Now* look at Tanya."

We did.

Tanya was in a position that would've been right for urinating in a drainage ditch.

"Born-again Christian," Pru told us.

Raf said, "This birth didn't work out either. She should try for one more."

"Ever been to Canada?" I asked Pru.

"Yes, and it's better, Paige. Better."

"But there are pinheads and child beaters and flag wavers up there as well."

"It's still better 'cause they're not Americans, and not from the fucking South, at least. I can deal with all the other shit if there's time," said Pru.

"I like a person with a goal," Raf said.

"Really? Well, then I wonder if you'd be real sweet and buy some drinks from me. It's gotta look like I been working to that pecker who runs the floor."

We ordered, and on her way to the bar Pru shot the banker fellow a hundred-watt smile.

———

"A person can be bad and still have a lot of courage," Raf
said in the car.
   "Bad?"
   "Yeah, very bad," he said.

RAF'S AMERICA

MOTORING over to Pru's in the smoke-colored car a day later, the radio amazed and impressed me with its clear delivery of the La Scala production of *Un Ballo in Maschera*. I liked this version, but knew enough Italian to get that the baritone was singing: "Three o'clock! Three o'clock! It's three, three, three, o'clock!"

" 'S really an honor, come in," Pru said.

Her apartment was in the art-gallery district; in an eighties' cake-shaped building that rose five layers tall. Wrapping each story were strips of chrome piping.

"This is my daughter, Lilith," Pru said, introducing a three-year-old well-nourished child with white-blond pigtails and ribbons. Lilith wore a long T-shirt that fitted her like a dress. "RICHARD HELL," the T-shirt said.

I crouched and shook her chubby hand.

Nearly the whole fourth floor of the round building was taken up by Pru's apartment. It had no interior walls. The place reminded me of a dance studio.

Back in the living area, pieces of cubistic furniture made a kind of corral, and there a wall of bookshelves showed hundreds of bright waxy spines.

"Dress codes are coming back strong in Texas schools. So's hair length," Pru was saying. "Now, having too-long hair can get you suspended from first grade."

"Probably Lilith won't be doing her schooling in Houston," I said. "Just a guess."

"It's the *home* of textbook adulteration. This is where they censor textbooks for the whole U.S.; the new home of book burning. People want Creationism taught in schools. The mugginess and stinking heat here ruined their brains a long time ago; parboiled these people's brains to shit. You can't think in places where there's no winter. I mean, consider California."

We lingered in the studio section at the front of the apartment. Here, wall-to-floor windows let everything be bathed by sun.

"You definitely make *out* at that job," I said.

"This place? Hell no. I fuck a married guy who owns the property so he charges me just utilities. Nothing for the layout."

"Well, right there, Pru . . ."

"Contempt!" she said.

"O.K., but how much *self*-contempt is involved?"

"Not one fuckin' drop."

She glided into the kitchen area, to a vast refrigerator with stainless-steel doors.

Her shorts—cut high and floppy—enhanced the shape and length of her legs. With the shorts, she wore a blue leotard.

"You want coffee, tea, or some kinda alcoholic drink? I got all politically correct beverage products. And I make my coffee and tea with bottled water, not that radon urine that runs from the tap."

Everywhere, unframed canvases were mounted on Pru's walls. They were big as Sunfish sails and featured males in Klan costumes. The Klansmen toted branding irons, dildos, flaming crosses. The eyeholes in their sheets smoldered a fluorescent red. Parts of flayed female carcasses—gray slashed-off limbs and trunks—littered the tar-black foregrounds of the paintings.

"My friend does those," Pru said. "She's talentless, of course, but, you know . . ."

Pru uncapped a jug of Polish water. "You realize you can no longer drink the tap water in most of the continental U.S.? Radon's *been* in the fuckin' ground but now they're admitting it's in the air and water supply. *It's* the cause of most internal cancers."

"Read the papers much?" I asked.

I had dropped onto a cube of couch in the living-room area.

Lilith wandered.

Pru arrived eventually, serving glasses of dark coffee that swam with chemical-free ice.

She folded up next to me, close on another piece of couch. She said, "The number one best school in Texas is a place where they teach girls to be contestants in beauty pageants. Guyrex it's called because it's run by two men."

"Whose names are Guy and Rex," I said.

"You fuckin' bet they are. The *worst* school, of course, is that fascist-front institution, Texas A and M."

I asked Lilith what she did with her days.

"Nothing," Lilith said.

Pru started in talking about witches, about the necessity of their role in early New England communities. "Everybody recognized they weren't witches, actually. Really, their function was *blame*," she said.

"I didn't know," I said.

Pru shrugged. "It was a way to deal with spinsters, 'cause unmarried women were threatening to a culture so small and so—you'd be astounded—so sexually active."

Her eyes, I noticed, were shaded cobalt-blue.

"And not that many witches were actually burned, actually," she said. "You probably know all this and you're humoring me."

I said I didn't. I hadn't heard Pru's version, anyway.

"How was it you met Raf?" I asked her.

"Riff-Raf? Oh, he and this guy I fuck—or, used to—Raymond Hollander. They picked me up from work one night after my car croaked. Raf was real sick but he was cool behind it—he *looked* good—and he was fun to talk to."

That was pretty much my own assessment of Raf, I supposed, except he wasn't always fun to talk to.

I had a meeting with an SHS administrator—Carla Cook.

I said, "Carla," but her focus stayed stuck on the memo before her.

Around her office, green and rhubarb-red plants exploded from macramé hangers. She had up a Wagner poster. Raspberry gulls flew off the rim of her teacup.

"Carla?" I said again.

"Let me interrupt you," she said, "or I'll lose the thought. To remind you about the president's picnic for the summer people. It's tonight, at five, in front of Lee Auditorium."

"Thank you," I said. "Now. As you know, I'm not working here anymore but you did promise to pay me up-top, although I learned the checks aren't being processed till mid-September. Also—doesn't matter now—but my parking decal and library card and swimming-pool pass still haven't come through."

Without glancing up, Carla handed over an envelope inscribed with my name. "That was left with us," she said.

Inside was a poem from Barny, the particle physicist. I lowered into an armchair to read the folded page.

In the cyclotron is shattered
Matter into antimatter
Straining meaning through a sieve
Till all the world's a negative.

"Sorry to appear rude, but don't settle in," Carla said. "Briefly let's just agree we won't enter anything into your work record, Mrs. Deveaux. We'll pretend nothing happened."

"With my class? Nothing did happen except one day they all decided they didn't want to write poetry anymore."

"I don't buy it," Carla said.

"I don't care, it's true."

"True," Carla said, without looking at me.

"You know it is," I said. "I know it is. Your ugly plants know. What's true is true."

Davey Salizar, who'd got me the conference job, said, "Maybe she was right."

"Shut up, Davey. For you the truth is whatever's hardest, most loathsome, and disagreeable."

"Those're starting points," he said.

We were perched on the front stoop at his house, which

was close to the Astrodome. He'd given me a can of luke-warm Lone Star beer.

We could hear Raf, skimming around inside Davey's dim parlor.

The sky was pink this evening and fuzzy with lights from the stadium. Gleaming cars, as if sweating in the sheen of dusk, filed off from an Astros game.

Raf appeared at last, dragging a square unpadded chair. He wrestled it out onto the porch stoop. "You despise comfort," he said to Davey.

"You bratty bastard. You've always had it too easy," said Davey.

"That's *not* true," I said, and I stuck up for Raf. I said he'd got into Princeton all on his own. That most of his high school classmates were truckers now or they worked for the local factory farm. That getting a Rhodes wasn't on just luck. "And since then, for nearly twenty years," I said, "he's taken the hardest jobs for the meanest pay. He could've chosen any of the twelve things he has a talent for, laid into that, and stacked up dough. Plenty of bosses' daughters have suggested the alternative. Sit still for money until Daddy dies; live in the Connecticut house they got as a wedding present; produce a couple kids; wear the suit; go golfing. And that's not even mentioning how now the divorcees are coming at him. . . ."

"You're no good for anything either," Davey said.

Raf said, "Of the many passers-by this hot evening, many have smiled at Paige. They enjoy seeing a pretty woman drinking beer on a Friday night."

I said, "One afternoon, a man phoned from New York. You know what he thinks I'm good for?"

"Worm dirt," Davey said.

"Nope, no. He said I'm good for twenty-five thousand

tax-free dollars. An arts grant from a reputable foundation."

Davey's shirt had no sleeves and as he punched chords on a portable keyboard veiny striations rose on his arms.

"Is this fact?" he asked.

"Twenty-five thousand. No strings," Raf said. "She don't even have to shred documents."

"That pisses me off," Davey said, resting the keyboard. "That makes me feel like vermin. With a *fraction* of that I could live well. I could buy an a.c., go to restaurants. Pay my rent and the light bill. I could put some down on a Yamaha synth or a four-track reel to reel. But I'm happy for you, Paige. I'm genuinely proud and happy. No I'm not."

"For *no* money, I could take a skillet to your skinny head," I told him.

Raf had the keyboard. He plunked around with it on his lap and now and then eased into intense musical scores.

"I never knew you could play," I said.

"Choir," Davey said dismissively.

"You are the mystery man," I said to Raf.

"I had a job bein' a mystery man for a while," he told us. "I was in this comic strip—remember *Brenda Starr*?"

Raf's vita—what a notion. He'd had all types of tough-guy jobs, the kind they build beer and shaving-razor ads around. He'd been a foundry worker. He was still a member of the steelworkers' union. And a waterman. He fished for lobster out of Seaforth, Mass., for a season. He'd been a smoke jumper in California, and a bouncer at the Las Vegas Sands. He had cut and hung sheet rock for a Baltimore apartment complex.

There was only one condition Raf put on accepting a job. He would sign on to any crew doing anything, provided he could get away with drinking while he worked. Risk or pay ran a faraway second place in his calculations.

He used to report home from the Baymoth Brass Foundry all slickered with sweat and a coat of filth—total blackface—and reeking even more of bourbon than of the roasted-metal foundry smell.

The fishing job was his worst. He had met the captain, a twenty-year-old father of three, in a Wasnascawa saloon. That was deep New England winter, and the next morning Raf had gone out on a ship called the *Tiger's Ass*.

Raf told me they hadn't been five minutes clear of the harbor, had just sighted Boston Light, when the kid captain said, "Bad wethah due, time to rock 'n' roll." Which meant break out the Irish.

Raf said there were no more woozy death-cheating days in his life than those he spent on the tilting frozen deck of the *Tiger's Ass*, trying to get the iced nets untangled with iced fingers.

"What nobody realizes," he said, "is those guys are sick all the fuckin' time. Puke sick all day, all night. Like when the bed's circling. That was everyday life, only if I fell off the whirling bed it was, you know, the watery-grave deal.

"Me and two wino Portuguese and the Irish kid, going out under hurricane warnings. The kid thought the Atlantic was like a freeway—chancy, but, what the fuck, let's go.

"We didn't know *what* we were doing. With the deck all greasy from the oil spraying outa the air compressor and engines. And everything with the stench of oil; whatever lunch you could force down or what you drank tasted of diesel. And every surface was already slippery from ice and seawater and drek and then *add* oil.

"It's not easy, getting good jobs where you can drink,"

said Raf. "It's gotta be so dangerous nobody normal would do it, or a job protected by some ferocious union, or so upper tier that nobody'd dare confront you. Like working in the White House, you could guzzle until your guts ignite. Or transportation. Sign onto a train crew, and goodbye sobriety. Smokin' shit and snorting. It's a marvel to me any train goes anywhere considering whose hand is on the switch and on the throttle. All aboard, you know?"

Raf's America.

I drove over to Pru's place almost every day, and she never exhausted her rantings. She had more than she could ever spend, really.

Lilith and I would get comfy on the cube chairs and listen to Pru's monologues and watch her perform her large startling life.

"Food!" she was saying now. "I mean, Americans are raised with a two-taste palate—sweet and salty. The only goddamn tastes they'll abide. No wonder I'm bulimic. Is it all right to tell you that? So what, I urp up after every meal. It's practically an act of conscience on my behalf. Cheeseburgers, for instance. They're sweet *and* salty. Because no one would eat the vile meat unless it was hidden under candied pickles and put on cakelike rolls."

"Cheeseburger," Lilith said to me.

"It's a political duty to vomit that meat. You know fast-food beef's all imported from rainforests that they've clear-cut for grazing land. And U.S. companies send the Third World all the pesticides that're too evil for use here. And that's *legal*. Then after everything's poisoned—rivers, topsoil, plants—whatever animals are left lying around dying, their flesh gets shipped back and made into cancer patties. I'd sooner drink a bucket of lead."

As she talked, Pru did dance moves and stretches, grasping and hanging from the rail bar in the studio section of her apartment.

"This machine, my body," she told us, "is my only means for getting the hell out of this country."

Her telephone rang twenty and thirty times a day.

She spoke into the receiver with a shy accommodating voice, and could work real-sounding giggles into her replies.

Twice, after phone calls, she asked me to watch Lilith. "Just while I dart out to see this guy," she said.

"I can't, I don't know how," I told Pru. "She could fall over, crack her head. She could die."

"No she'd never, Paige. You wouldn't hurt Lilith. She never needs anything. She's housebroken and all."

"I'll try it," I said.

Now Pru stood behind an ironing board pressing a black linen jumpsuit, starching it lightly from a pump-spray bottle.

I lay across two cube chairs and lit a cigarette. "Never *ever* smoke," I said to Lilith.

"Radon'll do her in first. Or the hole in the ozone layer and the drought and famine it'll bring," Pru said. "The greenhouse effect's already happening. She might as well smoke."

Pru backed up from the ironing board, pointed one of her legs up behind her and brought her foot to her shoulder blade.

She said, "Something I'd love to do is be a Dallas Cowboy cheerleader. I mean, just for a single game. I'd drop my panties, do a hundred-and-eighty-degree bend-over, moon the whole fuckin' city of Dallas. And I'd wait for a nationally televised game—a Monday nighter—to do it."

Brahms played on Pru's radio now—solemn music that swirled like steam.

The phone sounded. Lilith stayed a statue. I fidgeted for four rings, preparing to answer.

"Pru there?" a fellow said.

"No, she isn't. May I tell her who called?"

"Buddy. I'll try again later," the man said. "Or just tell her Buddy, and it's room two-oh-seven."

I pictured Buddy, hopeful, his heart thudding, his throat dry; scrubbed and brushed and waiting in a Houston hotel.

I wanted to phone him back and tell him, don't wait; that I knew Pru and that he shouldn't bother.

But I could never be certain about anyone—what she or he would do next.

I was babysitting Lilith, but she didn't want to go anywhere or do anything, or even chat.

We napped together on Pru's futon, and I had a dream of somewhere with goldenrods swaying and the wind smelling of burnt-orange autumn. The dream place was like those in my father's paintings, one of his depictions of heaven.

When I awoke, I asked Lilith if I had said anything in my sleep. She remembered I had said, "Thanksgiving," and now I remembered that I'd forgiven her, but I never could think what for.

"Pru is a *billboard*," Raf said. "A screaming ad for herself."

"I like her, though."

He said, "I warn you, if you haven't already sensed this, that she's a person who *wants* things. She'll flatter you, and flirt with you, but that woman's got a program."

"Couldn't want anything from me."

"Oh, the hell. Maybe she wants to go back to school and thinks you can get her into Harvard. Or that you can get *her* poetry published. Maybe you're the ideal babysitter. Or—this is the most likely—once you're convinced that she's your friend, she'll try to grab me away from you, which she's dead sure she can do anytime she halfway feels like it."

We were in the dining room. Opened on the round-top table was Cioran's *The Trouble with Being Born*. I noticed where Raf had marked his place and when he loped off for a glass of water I read: "We should have abided by our larval condition, dispensed with evolution, remained incomplete, delighting in the elemental siesta and calmly consuming ourselves in an embryonic ecstasy."

When he returned, I said, "I am so glad I'm not *you!*"

"I can tell you Pru sent an MX missile into Raymond's life a couple years ago."

"She told me."

"Her version," Raf said, flapping shut the Cioran book.

Often he read with his blind eye closed, squinting as if focusing a camera. Whenever I saw this, I thought he was more serious than other readers, more engaged, and more exacting.

"It was simple hit and run, according to her," I said. "Only they *both* ran, because Raymond didn't cotton to Pru's politics and she isn't liable to change. That was that."

"Well, interesting," Raf said. "Raymond took it all a little more to heart. He was torn into a billion fuckin' pieces, in fact. He filed for divorce. Only right then Luisa announced that she was pregnant. Raymond nearly ate from a gun over the whole deal, and he is *still* in shreds over Pru."

"Huh," I said.

"You know that night he and I picked her up from work? I was red-eyed total but even dumped I could tell she was scary. She was all over me like a fuckin' nightshirt. And not because she wanted me but because that's what she *does*. And. Also. Because it ripped Raymond up to see her acting like that. She enjoys ripping people up, for all her save-the-whales talk."

I said, "She's confused, I think. You'd *have* to be confused to work in one of those stripper places."

"She's a fuckin' rapist!" Raf said.

From Pru's studio I saw sunset clouds tinted copper. Down in the courtyard the water in the frog pond looked like iodine.

Pru and I were going on a double date.

She wore a white satin mini dress, satin mules. Her shampooed hair smelled of coconut.

Now she was mixing up her own cologne. I saw vanilla extract go in, and rose water, a tiny piece of orange peel. "Whales die for perfume," she said. "The oil. And makeup, you know they drip that shit into bunnies' eyes until they see how much'll blind them."

"On this you should talk to my mom," I said. "She once arm-cleared a shelf and pitched all my makeup because of it."

"Atta girl. Excellent woman," said Pru.

"And last Christmas she gave me the full line of Paul Penders, because they don't animal-test at all. Good old Dottie. She can outdrink Raf and still seem her normal self. Of course, her normal self isn't normal."

Pru said, "You'd think I'd end up smelling like fruitcake with these ingredients. But no, the scent makes men hungry. They're always getting their appetites confused. One guy I know—are you listening?"

"Hard," I said.

"He's worth jillions and never worked a minute of his gross sinful life, but the only way he can do it is if there's chocolate food messed in. Like Hershey's syrup? Sex, I mean."

"Huh," I said. "Let's change the channel."

"Symbolic as all hell to me, Paige."

"It is, but a well-traveled road. Where oh where is your babysitter?"

I answered the door for the sitter, who stepped inside but said nothing. The woman had stripped her hair of all color, and her complexion, by lack of contrast, looked doughy, drowning-victim white.

"Portuguese," Pru whispered to me.

"One of the undead. Drawn by Brueghel. On return from hell," I said.

Pru had worked me into a cocktail dress of hers. I'd brought no evening clothes to Houston.

"Looks better on you, you should keep it," she kept saying.

I thought for wearing in public this silk dress needed

more substance. It seemed an underslip, not a dress. And the sheer black nylons and garter belt—also Pru's—went with my notion of whore.

"Hell, it's all from New *York*," she said, as she stuck brass hoop earrings and a brass cuff on me. "Classy, classy. What size are your feet?"

Her size, so now I teetered on six-inch heels: shoes that were open-toed, sequin-sprinkled, covered with an iridescent fabric.

"You oughta dress that way all the time. You know, I love putting clothes on other women. I mean, *love* it. Do you think that means I'm a latent gay?"

"Big furious no," I said.

"Especially if they're pretty. Then I like to watch them in action and see the effects of the clothes. And I have fantasies . . ." Pru said.

"All woman do, probably."

"And I've watched movies of other women in bed."

"Let me guess," I said. "Your fantasies were better."

"Yeah, but what does that prove? Fantasies always are."

"You'd know it by now if you were gay."

"Raf told me that you are," Pru said.

"He what?"

"Bisexual. He said you're bisexual. He said the three of us should go to bed together sometime, is all. Don't get mad at him, Paige. If you're mad, it'll spoil tonight."

Raf and Raymond were our dates. They were already late.

Pru's pride in my appearance made her as loopy as a mom who'd wrestled her daughter away from a swim meet and into Easter whites. "Look at you!" she said. "Raf sees you, he's gonna pop his cork."

———

Pru opened the door on a lopsided Raf. His elbow on the side wall was all that kept him standing.

He wore a new suit with a fish-scale sheen. The shirt underneath was peacock blue, and where buttons belonged it had a zipper, unzipped.

"Two beautiful girls without mercy," he said. " '. . . Her foot light, her eyes wild.' "

"That's beautiful, Raf," Pru said.

I said Keats had thought so.

Pru said, "Raf, you look like a low rider!"

"Low as you go. Another great thing about Houston is that the humidity glazes everything with STP."

"We're first worst for air, third worst for ozone damage," Pru said. "Where's Raymond?"

I said, "He probably refused to be seen with a guy in Raf's clothes."

"Thank you, Paige. I wanted something in a snakeskin pattern . . ."

"To match your soul."

"Thank you again. But all they had left was this sardine fabric. Now, did you wanna ask me a question, Paige? The answer's yes."

"Yes, you had a little slip?"

"The way you two look I could eat both your little slips," Raf said. "Raymond'll be here in a second. He's crawling along. Yes, we hurt ourselves with the malt that wounds."

"Not Raymond! Not after three years!" I said.

"We'll both pay tomorrow, but let's nobody ruin tonight."

Pru stepped past Raf and into the hall. "Bleeding Jesus, Raf wasn't kidding!" she said.

I leaned to see. Raymond was on hands and knees, crawling along the hallway in a suit that was the twin of Raf's.

"This is too much. What do you suppose is on TV?" I said.

"Come on, give the boys a chance," Pru begged.

"Yeah, give us that," said Raf.

I said, "No. I and a Portuguese voodoo woman are going to babysit Lilith and watch television together. We're going to watch *Divorce Court*. These guys—one of them can't stand, and the other can just barely! Besides that, they're both dressed in oven wrap!"

"I can so stand. It's that I lost somethin' valuable and I'm searching for it," Raymond yelled.

"And what did you lose, Raymond? Your wedding ring?" I asked.

"How'd you find that out? Raf, did you tell her?"

"Nope," said Raf. "I guess you're just not a very complicated cowpoke, Ray-mo."

"You call me Ray-mo one more time and I swear I'll beat you to death," Raymond said.

"Ray-mo," said Raf.

Even crawling and in the sparkling pimp suit, Raymond's anger was impressive.

Raf said, "Ray-mo, let's say we behave so the girls don't lock us out."

"Why would they lock us out, they got a union shop? I didn't mean that, Pru! I hope you don't take a slander from it. Raf? Help me find my wedding ring and I'll kill you a little later."

Raf ambled over and fell down. "Fair deal," he said.

"Ain't gonna be a lotta help on your back," Raymond said.

I said, "Pru, do you see what tonight'll be like? We might

make it out of here by dawn, but they'll have lost the car keys."

"Holy mother, I did leave the keys in the car! Can you believe that?" Raymond said.

Raf was laughing and Raymond said, "Paige, you're gonna be a widow. I can't stop myself from killing him now."

"Or I'll kill him," I said. "Then I'll be a murderer widow watching TV with a toddler and a dead woman from the Azores. What bothers me most is I spent time getting dressed up for this."

"You look wonderful," Raymond said. "And, Pru? I'm in love with you and I should face up to it. That ain't the bottle talking neither."

I told Raf to stand up. "And zip your shirt!" I said.

"You wanna fuck?" he asked me. "I'll do things to you nobody's thought of."

"Who could *refuse* that offer?" I said.

Pru asked, "What's left that nobody's thought of? I'm just curious."

"If Paige answers no, Prudence, how about you?" said Raf.

"You married a maggot," she told me.

"A one-eyed dead one," Raymond said.

Raf said, "Let's load up in the limo. I got dancin' feet and a pantsload of penis."

"Oh, ugh," Pru said.

"O.K., fuck the wedding ring, fuck my marriage. Raf's right. Let's just get goin'," Raymond said.

Pru asked me if we should.

Both men were up now, brushing each other off, trying to behave.

"We'll just pretend they have a disease, Paige. That's what the AMA considers alcoholism," Pru said.

"True, but they also consider rabies a disease, yet I rarely go dancing with two rabid men."

"Pru wishes she had four rabid men, or an auditoriumful," Raf said. "Or an army of rabid men. Rabbit men?"

Raymond said, "Just please don't let no one have stolen the car."

The summer Raf loved someone else, I kept thinking, "That's some other Raf." And mostly I was thinking how to work the next curve, so hard was a single Cameroon day.

At the Pilot, the water supply would shut off. We'd bargain for soap, carry cakes of it around in the pockets of our trousers. And then mornings we'd check to see if the sprinklers were out on the lawns of the couple–few government buildings.

In a hard jet of the sprinkler water we could shampoo our hair, wash our clothes, rinse Mario's painting jars and brushes, soak our sneakers through and through.

The arches of sprinkler water and their mist would make great white shapes that looked like shrubbery from a distance. Whenever he saw the shapes appear, Mario would say, "Problem solved, Piagga," or he'd say, "We got the luck!"

As we were leaving Pru's, I copped a fifth of Benedictine from her liquor cabinet.

"Sit up straight, woman. Drink with dignity," Raf told me, as we sped in Pru's car through a tunnel of smeary lights, past a candelabra-like fountain.

Raymond lounged sideways on the passenger's seat, gaping at Pru.

The drink finally caught fire in my stomach. "Where is she taking us?" I asked.

"You'll like it," Pru said.

Raymond said, "I can make trivial decisions. Like is it Pepsi-Cola or RC; what watt of bulb goes in this fixture. But I'll be switched if I can decide who to love, or what God wants."

"Knock it off, Ray-mo," Raf said. "You're fast descending the ladder of my respect."

The downtown streets were deserted. Lights were on for no one in the high stacks of mirrory towers. But the avenues away from the business district were packed with traffic, and there were men heckling cars from curbs, night people soliciting. Neon bathed everything deep candy colors—reds, purples, oranges, greens.

"I brought this up with my sponsor," Raymond said. "Leandra. She had me read Exodus, where Moses gets the big ten. So I'm studying them and for the most they're straight out—don't rob, don't kill. But you know the one God gets most het up about? 'Keep holy the Sabbath!' Like, you've *had* your six days to work. Go on break!"

"You don't sound too squashed anymore, Raymond," Pru said.

"My head is kinda clearing. Can I have a sip from your bottle, Paige? It won't make anything worse. I've already fallen, committed the sin of sloth, I believe it is."

Pru took us to a gallery opening.

We moved in a weavy procession up a gravel walkway, past security guards, into a lobby that was wide, white, icy with marble.

"David Salle," Raf said to a painting. "My, you smell."

Maybe a hundred people milled about inside the main

hall. Pru swept from person to person. She kissed rouged cheeks, received hugs from the men.

Raymond seemed blunted now and stood out of her sphere.

Raf had located a bay of hot snacks. He and I set to work on them.

"You're eating all the shrimp puffs," I said.

"*You* ate all the caviar disks and there were thousands."

"What may I get you?" asked a bartender.

Sculptures were on exhibit: nine-foot columns of white-enameled steel.

Raf decided he liked the columns and that they meant a great deal. He asked me if I could see how much they meant.

"Ah, not sure," I said.

"They have to do with narration," he said.

"Oration? Oration, yes. Possibly they do."

"They're guideposts to a signified infinity," he said. "That's what's important."

Pru introduced us to the artist, a professor of hers back when she was at Rice.

He was short, with an angel-hair toupee, a black turtleneck, black slacks.

"All the shrimp puffs are gone!" he said. "These people are vultures."

"Come," said Pru, and drew me away to a showy washroom.

A black woman had been hired to sit watch in here. She seemed an installation of scorn. She wore a crisp tailored uniform and a paper hat pinned to her hair.

"What am I supposed to do?" Pru asked.

"About what?" I said. "Raymond?"

"I didn't ask him to love me. I didn't say, 'Leave your wife and kid.' And I *sure* don't want you mad at me, Paige.

But suddenly Raf's decided I'm home-wrecking scum. And yet, just before we came in here, Raymond grabbed me and went, 'Let's do it all. Fuck it. Let's go for broke.' "

"Get married he means? I don't know, Pru. Raymond's awfully drunk. Why don't we just play through tonight and say it doesn't count? Nothing that happens tonight goes on anybody's scorecard."

Pru got a Raggedy Ann doll look of helplessness and hurt.

She pulled me to her and gave me a trembling embrace. "Please don't turn on me," she said, her cheek warm on mine.

I stepped back, aware of the attendant's view of our runners-up-in-a-beauty-contest hug, and leaned my shoulders against a brilliant tile wall. I lifted and flexed both my feet, which were straining from the steep arch of the borrowed high heels.

Pru was examining her mirror image. She smoothed the satin over her stomach; tugged the skirt, adjusted it on her hips.

"A lot of these people here hate me because they invested in my daddy and he got rich on their dough and blew. They think I'm just a climber and that I should've left town with him. Even Lilith's father pulled out on me."

"So you're kind of like Trish Nixon still hanging around D.C. after Watergate," I said.

"Don't compare me to a Republican, but yeah. I come to these festivities out of contempt. To goad the men, spook the women. You're the last *woman* friend I have, Paige. And now Raymond's jeopardizing that, and Raf's poisoning your ears. You want Raymond, don't you? That's what's really bothering you."

"Even if I did, Pru, that package is wrapped up and ribbon tied and your name's on it."

We were in the cosmetic-repair area now, where, at a vanity counter, two older women balanced on rotating stools, their chins raised as they curved lipsticks on their O-shaped mouths.

Pru seized me with both hands, seized my shoulders. "We can *fix* it with Raymond so that it's you he wants!"

"No, no," I said.

"You *don't* want Raymond then?" She shook me by the shoulders and woggled me on the high-heel sticks.

"No," I said, and the word came out in three wavy syllables.

"I'm sorry. Jeez-oh, I jiggled off one of your fake eyelashes," Pru said.

"Raymond's married, and I'm married," I said. "And besides, he and Raf are best friends."

"Since when?" Pru said. She hitched up the skirt of her satin mini and straightened her garter-belt straps.

"Since when *which*?"

"Any of it," Pru said, rehooking her nylons.

On my cheek a black mothlike thing batted with each blink—the fake lash.

I found Raf explaining the sculptor's work to the sculptor.

The artist's hairpiece seemed askew, as if Raf's tirade had blown the thing sideways.

"How're we doing?" I asked Raf.

"I must go," the sculptor said. He touched Raf's wrist. "Keep thinking."

We nudged through the clusters of art patrons, who were sun-darkened and perfumed and whose gleaming jewelry struck sparks.

We caught up with Raymond. He and a man in a fringed suede coat were talking outdoor lore.

"I'm in a fifteen-foot boat out on Alligator Bayou with Ole Mossy. Dusk," Raymond said. "He tells me we're steering by the cypress shapes—they're just these black formations but Mossy's got 'em all memorized. It smells like snake and all we can make out is egrets."

"You see 'em even if there's no *moon*," said the man in the suede coat.

"Aren't they *white*? And I'm saying, 'Mossy, maybe we could hang it *up* at this point?' "

"Mossy never wants to go home, though."

"No, and the bugs are having a smorgasbord," Raymond said.

"They don't bite *him*," said the man in suede.

"That's right, they never bite him. Hello, Paige," Raymond said. "We're just trading stories about Ole Mossy."

Raf said, "I lost all my money on him once in the Preakness. He sprained a fetlock or something and had to be put down."

"This is Paige Deveaux," Raymond said. "And the funny one's Raf, her husband."

"He *looks* funny," said the man in suede.

"Call me Deadeye," Raf said.

"I'm Danny Hail and that's my son. He don't talk." The man in suede thumbed toward a fellow with sorrowful eyes, a tight smile. "That's Paul, but he don't talk."

"Pleasure to meet you both," I said.

Raymond said, "Ole Mossy's a Cajun, got a hunting lease on some land over in Louisiana? *The* hunting lease, just about. He's perfect for a guide but once he's started he won't stop."

"He'll say to you something like 'Thought you wanted to *hunt*,' " said the man in suede.

"Yeah, that Ole Mossy," Raf said. "He mows down some wildlife and strayed domestic pets and eats a mess of crayfish and drinks from his radiator and finally ambles on back to his lean-to and curls up for the night with his pappy or his ma."

"You know all about him," the man in suede said.

Raymond said, "Raf's from the enlightened North. Everything all right with Prudence?" he asked me.

It was midnight. The Ole Mossy stuff I heard Raf saying was the last I heard from him before he fell off the earth.

TUNNEL OF AIR

A L O N E at the house with things Raf had gathered—bookshelves, two braided rugs, a cracked bust of Eurydice, other oddments—I huddled in a chair, my eyes fixed on the corner, a globe there.

For dawn there had been angry clouds, startling winds, a tropical storm coming from Corpus. A frog quacked. The cicadas made a constant sound—it didn't go anywhere or do anything; it did not beat like a heart. More than being hot and tired and scared about Raf, the sound made me miss my parents, miss boredom, miss TV.

"I hate him," I told the globe, but that felt a lot like hating myself.

I counted to a thousand, counted back, thousands of times.

I kept picturing Raf on top of some twenty-year-old.

Around noon, I called Brookline hoping his drunkenness had put him on a plane and taken him home. In my ear was the tiny rattling of that phone's ring. I hung up and redialed, hung up, redialed. I ate a pretzel, dialed again.

I called my mother—not answering—and now my father, in Providence. I told him that Raf had vanished.

"Big deal," Mario said.

I read from my notebook something I'd got from Barny, the physicist. "What keeps quarks together are gluons, a kind of quanta, that're *not real particles.*"

When the Palm was open, I walked there and sat; sat watching a stain on the boards of the dance floor.

I remembered that before Cameroon, Raf had said, "Don't make pictures in your head, Paige. You can't guess how I am with her. You'd be wrong."

Walking home, the brown clouds took on animal shapes and started marching. Female voices sounded a chantlike hymn from the Desglaises church. The air burned to breathe. I'd been awake for so long I was logy, drunklike.

There were lashes of wind suddenly, and trees plunging, crooked lines of rain. I slugged along, bent, the wind cutting down on me; light-headed from sleeplessness and the heat, and from the rain, stinging.

Life would go like this, I knew—days, weeks, a month, two.

"Swallowed my chew gum," Raymond said. "You know, it was a compliment, Raf choosin' me for a friend. I brought him here from Baton Rouge that summer with all the falling stars? Can't remember what we were *doin'* then, but it musta been disgusting." Raymond staggered and caught a door jamb with his free hand. He stood there, propped, wagging his head. "No worse than this recent. Prudence tell you she found me trying to roll up under the car last night to sleep? A drunk runs off and hides 'cause he knows he's caught in it. Ashamed of being that depressed, like it's got its own stench. He sees people doing the day-to-day, walking around. . . . 'S like everyone else moves by in some trance."

A terrarium night with steam at rooftop level. The black sky was low. I could make out, from the porch, the St. Francis birdbath and could smell the sticky fruit droppings from the tree in the clinic's yard.

In my notebook I wrote,

> *old red air*
> *fine needles for a tattoo*
> *whump and oom-pah*
> *of the rained-on corner band.*

Raymond's white shirt was all the way unbuttoned. He went to urinate in the side yard.

"How'd *you* meet Raf?" he called back to me.

I hesitated before answering. "He was this guy Nick's friend," I said.

"Nick?"

"I lived with him before Raf."

"Huh," Raymond said, as he returned. "Nick a *good* friend of Raf's?"

"Real good friend," I said.

"So, how'd he act when you shifted over?"

"Relieved," I said.

"That ain't true," Raymond said, smiling.

Now the night was gone. The headlights on a passing city bus blinked off. Sunrise took the sky through grays, reds, oranges, up to a cyan blue.

I walked Raymond inside. I fixed a breakfast of bread,

and coffee, a bowl of carrot salad with coconut and carob shavings.

The linoleum in the kitchen was silty. The soles of our shoes scratched and whispered.

Raymond didn't eat, didn't sit. He stood with his back to the screen door.

Behind him, in the yard out there, were Raf's plantings: a flower garden of begonia, periwinkle, and some yarn-ball blossoms called "Sparkle verbena."

"Am I in your notebooks?" Raymond asked.

"You?" I said. "Oh, sure, you. You're at the heart of it all."

He pulled me to him, sighed into my hair. I felt him harden against my thigh. He said, "Raf'll be back and this time he'll find you."

"Yeah. Probably that's the idea."

Raymond said, "*My* idea I'm havin' right now is—though not new—right now it seems a real good, border-line-genius idea."

"Don't," I said. "Not yet."

Pru wore a sleeve of pink fabric, like a playsuit of Lilith's; no underwear. Her short hair was twisted into thorns.

She was working with a piece of pine board and woodcut tools. She pried loose a jagged line of wood, across the grain, cracked the gouge handle with a hammer.

She said to Raymond, "You hate my doing this."

"Hadn't noticed," he said.

"But if you *had*, you'd hate it."

"Depends," said Raymond.

"No," Pru said. "You would. For some reason, any goddamned reason."

Raymond said, "Paige wasn't noticing you either. She's focused someplace else. She's just too polite to say."

"Then go live with her!" said Pru. "See how long she can stand you."

"Say, Paige. Pru says I should go live with you."

"She doesn't even mind your drunk talk. The same fuckin' note, over and over."

"Say, Paige, Pru says I should live with you and you like my one-note drunk talk."

"Only *he* doesn't like sex, Paige, you should know. He doesn't *dis*like it, but he can go weeks . . ."

"Paige doesn't care," said Raymond.

I said, "Could we change the subject, please? I mean to anything at all?"

"One note, one note, one note," said Pru.

"Right after he left Princeton," said Raymond, "I stayed with Raf in Malibu. He's living on the beach. Tex Watson's his landlord. And Raf'd fight with him and fight with Manson. This's before they were into killing people, but just doing goats, drinking the blood of live chickens, I think I heard.

"Another time, a little baby shark floats up in the tide? And this girl with Raf, she wants to keep it. Dead little silver shark. But by next day the whole entire beach's polluted so Raf's gotta bury the thing. Pru thinks I'm gay," Raymond said.

"I tend to think that about most men," she said. She turned to me. "Except, that time at work when Raf walked in. I'd never seen him before. One look at him and I felt weak."

Raymond said, "I better sign myself into Ben Taub, they got a detox. 'Cause it's getting like 'Wonder whose place this is, sure looks familiar.' You know? I mean, how do you *steer* the goddamn thing?"

Raymond called on me after the hospital—browner, blonder, thinner; even more tightly wound than before.

It was late October, a melancholy, thick, itchy day.

"You wanna know what I think?" he asked. He had a duffel bag of Raf's hooped in his arms.

The smoke-colored car was loaded up with Raf's stuff —his running gear, his pairs of black Levi's, his shaving kit, his T-shirts, a carved stone jaguar, his books, swollen and broken from the way he read them. All this was packed into three labeled boxes, going back to Brookline by rail.

Raymond bent into the car with Raf's CD player and CD's. The interior was an oven from the sun at the end of the drive.

"Yes, I do," I said. "Want to know what you think."

"Raf's like me. I mean, he's not anything but *roach* for leaving you behind, but otherwise he's just wobbly and can't trust what he thinks or sees. He's not running from you, he's just running."

Whenever Raf came to mind these days, I felt Sunday-morning stuff—queasy, hungover, sore from the bones out. Sometimes I wished he'd never happened.

After the train station and dropping Raf's boxes, we drove onto the Loop and off, into a city of malls, plazas, department stores, garages, all expensive-looking and pin-neat.

"I'm about to change your life," Raymond said, as I followed him into a place called MicroBytes.

In here were cool gray plastic and beige Plexiglas and books that looked plump and promising but were written in math.

"I'm buying you a computer, Paige, what they call a laptop? It's a kind you carry around, size of a briefcase, and there's programs that go with it that'll teach you what to do."

"Raymond, I can't let you. Thanks, but, between Pru and Luisa . . ."

"Aw, the hell with 'em. Pru's fine, and I been fightin' with her all day anyway. And I left Luisa everything—the ranch, our daughter, the VCR. She's got a new boyfriend she has to impress—our lawyer. Says she needs it all. I don't mind. Hell, I like paring down. You know what else?"

"What?"

"It's a wide old world," Raymond said, and sighed.

On the round dining table now were the machine, a printer, printout sheets, a half-dozen manuals, program boxes, a mouse and textured mouse pad, black-ink ribbons, a power bar and surge suppressor, unopened plastic-wrapped packets of floppy disks. All like a question I hadn't heard myself ask.

Pru and Raymond took me out into their night, which included dinner at the Camellia, a pink place off the Eastex Freeway; ale for me and Pru at a jazz club called Lapaz; drinks in a dance cellar.

There Raymond hauled me onto the amber-lit floor. He pressed a hand in the small of my back and moved me around with all the strength he'd got from carrying bricks or steel or house parts around in the sun for so many years.

"The best feeling," he told my right ear, "is when you don't give a fuck. Lately, I don't."

"You've got Raf in there moving your mouth," I said.

Pru and I decided to walk over to the Palm. We cut through an alley behind Stonewall Elementary. Coming the other way was a man in a suit and fedora, his arm around his young son.

As we got close, Pru nudged me. "Watch," she said.

She unbuttoned her top and flapped open the right side, baring her breast entirely.

The man lowered his eyes. With a firm hand, he gripped his son's head, forcing the aim of the boy's face away.

We walked on. Pru giggled as she buttoned up. The sound of her tinkling laugh sent me back to junior high, slumber parties, night whispers, the TV with the sound off, homemade cake.

"Got weekend custody," Raymond said, introducing me to his old dog, Connie. The dog was a pencil-faced collie with a brushed coat of butterscotch and white. She stood balanced sideways on the rear seat of Raymond's big convertible.

Downtown, he parked at a meter. This was a Saturday but he bought tomorrow's paper for me from a girl in a cap.

I followed him into a lobby with marble floors, brass door fittings, live plants. The building had a postal drop where Raymond collected a week's worth of his mail— bundles of mail, rolled and rubber-banded.

"Could try Galveston Beach," he said, when we were back in the car. "Me and Raf used to go when it got too

hot for him in Houston. And coeds still show up on week-
ends hoping to grab a last-minute tan."

"Sounds like Raf's song. But what would we say if we
found him?" I asked.

"We won't," Raymond said.

He had his painter's radio, a slim black plastic beatbox,
positioned on the dash. At Galveston, the radio picked up
a program of garage-band hate music, and the speakers
sounded with brittle crunch and din. "I'm Lisa," the d.j.
said. "Bringing you 'Hell Comes to Your House,' like it
or not."

Raymond jerked the wide steering wheel with both fists,
maneuvering among pedestrians and double-parked cars.

Beautiful teenagers idled everywhere. They perched on
cars and on curbs, leaned, looking glazed, against store-
fronts or affectionately on one another.

We drove to a beach slum away from the main strip,
where the day's buttery light cast wet-looking reflections
on rooftops and ramshackle housing.

Raymond squinted around as we drifted along a street
called Valparaiso. He let the car skid onto a gravel berm
before a three-story with mud-green siding.

He climbed easily from the car, breathed a great breath,
lit a cigarette.

I noticed this and that—a boy writing on a rock; a
souped-up race car aboard a trailer behind a convenience
store; a woman pedestrian wearing only a bathrobe; the
sound of a car with no muffler; kids rushing from house
to house, ringing doorbells, hiding in shrubs.

Raymond walked Connie and fed her a bowl of dried
dogfood. She clambered back into the convertible as he
sauntered up to the door of the three-decker.

The woman he spoke with wore rimless glasses and ragtag Army fatigues. Her hair was mostly buzz cut but here and there had stubby braids. "It doesn't bother *me*," I heard her say. "But, see, you brought someone along, and, Raymond? We would never bring someone along if we came to see you, would we? And what is she, anyway, a hitchhiker? Jesus."

Raymond leaned in to answer and, after a beat, the woman said, "O.K., misunderstood. Sorry. So maybe he was in and out of here, but over a month ago. Only I didn't tell you that, right? And juiced, like he just came to argue. I mean, the man's confused. You ought to do something about him before somebody else does, you know? 'Cause I mean the mouth on that guy . . ."

Raymond stopped the car by a tidepool and let Connie out for a stretch. The water was seething with snakes. Raymond threw a stick in and the water swallowed the stick.

"That was a bust, 'cept we know he's alive. I had my toes crossed he'd be there," Raymond said.

"What a scary woman," I said.

"Patton? Nah. Her and her satellites got a gay bar in town, and they'll always take Raf in, he happens through. On pity, they *say*, but they enjoy bickerin' with him because he's on their level. Connie, get back in the car, girl."

"He fights with them about being lesbians?"

"No, no. It's that they're—they want their own country—what it comes down to. And religion, he'll get 'em on, like there's one tryin' to start up a ministry."

I nodded.

Leaving Galveston, we saw the last light burnishing the city. In moments, the downtown was a few black buildings set before a copper sky. We didn't talk much on the return.

———

"Need I remind you, when you go to buy your turkey, stay away from factory farmed," my mother said over the phone.

"It can't be Thanksgiving time," I said.

Dottie said, "Did they stop putting lithium in the water supply? You're the second person I've talked to who doesn't know what day it is."

A silver steady rain played in the leaves, brightened them and waxed their little bit of color. The rain drummed on the windows. I lay on the vinyl couch staring at the hand printing on a white postcard, which read,

> Paige,
>   They ought to change the fucking symbol for infin-
> ity. Instead of an eight on its side it should be o—
> Zero (Nothing).

Barny, the physicist, hadn't sent this card as I had thought on first read. It was from Raf. There was no signature, but I knew Raf had sent it.

The card had a Wasnascawa postmark, a part of Boston's South Shore near where my mother lived at the Seahorse Inn.

Now I had the shakes so bad my teeth locked. I ripped the card in half, squared the halves, ripped them into quarters.

From the back door I flung the pieces at Raf's garden.

I fetched the pieces and began taping them together, but they were damp, limp.

This seemed an idle rain, although another storm was

tearing up from the tropics—this time, a hurricane named Hilda—the radio warned.

A silhouette appeared at the screen door. Dark-shadowed, Raymond looked hard-carved and hungry.

"You gonna let me in, Paige? Lemme in," he said.

"I don't know. Are you alone?"

"I'm alone," he said. "Open it."

"You brought the devil with you, didn't you? I hear him snapping at your heels."

I tucked Raf's postcard away, deciding.

"What'll happen if I do?" I asked. "Bad, bad, bad?"

"Wouldn't be, unless you wanna put that construction on it." He glanced down at his wristwatch. "We got until seven forty-five, a.m. Then I'd have to shower and get out of here and drive to work."

"The door isn't locked," I said.

IN THE
CYCLOTRON

THE KNEES were blown out of my Levi's and the shoe-laces missewn through the eyelets of my boots. In Baton Rouge I'd bought the boots and a cold-weather canvas anorak.

Flooding storms had hit here and a watch for Hurricane Hilda was on.

Lawns were ponds; highways were rivers.

My motel stood on high ground in McComb, Missis-sippi. The room had a scarlet bed quilt, globe lamps, a lizard on the glass door; a Bible subtitled *Revised Standard Version*. The walls were like wet taffy, high-glossed an ivory white.

On the color TV now, a hurricane expert answered viewer calls.

People were giddy. Rules had been suspended. Maids and their children frolicked clothed in the pool.

I lay in bed. On the night table were a bottle of Grey Riesling, and the Good Book, and my ticking timepiece.

The flood's noise thrashed on the roof—more wind and water.

The TV man switched to talking about light. He said the waves reaching us had traveled all the way from galaxies in Andromeda Nebula or they'd come from Hydra, two thousand million light-years off.

Through the one front window, I saw low violet clouds, black pines, a slip of freeway.

I read from Ecclesiastes:

Emptiness, emptiness . . . everything is empty. All things are wearisome, more than one can say.

I *had* bought the boots, whenever that was. Now I dragged from bed and, crouching on the tufted carpeting, put a fist into each. That cheered me up for a few sweeps of the second hand. I stayed on the carpet, holding the boots and staring at them.

I waited to phone Raymond until I thought Pru was on shift at her job. But I got that wrong. Pru answered.

"You cunt! You fucked Raymond!" she said.

"I know," I said.

"You whoring cunt . . . !"

"Please, Pru. Just let me say something to him."

"No. Anyway he's not here. I *liked* you!"

"I liked you too. I'm sorry. It was all wrong . . . very, very wrong . . . completely. I hoped no one would find out."

"Are you kidding me? Raymond's never acted *happier*. He's talking about dividing his time between here and there, living half with me, half with you."

"But I'm not *there*, I've left. I'm going home. Not home but, I mean—Massachusetts."

Pru said, "You mean you fucked Raymond and moved

away? No goodbye, or nothing? This must have Raf in it. Is he there with you?"

"No, no, I'm alone. Listen, I won't bother calling again. If you'd just please tell Raymond . . ."

"It's all right, I'm not mad anymore. You should call back. You should turn around and *come* back, the way you sound, Paige, which is scary."

Stepping out into the Mississippi dawn, the fog was warm and pearl-gray around me. It seemed so palpable I thought I could just part it, make an aisle for myself from the motel door to the car.

Marshes spread with algae wallowed on either side of the asphalt road. This was Winona, halfway between Jackson and Memphis. Beyond the marshes and going on forever was swamp, bitter black swamp, speared with a thousand headless trees; jaggedy stumps, as though their tops had been ripped away. A sign nailed to one said: PAPAW'S CAT-FISH! Another read: PREPARE TO MEET GOD.

In my dreams, I stepped out a window and fell down a tunnel of air. I plummeted stiff, straight arms and legs, so that a woman watching said at first she thought I was a store mannequin falling. I landed on a Caterpillar diesel generator involved with street repair. Nothing looked broken, the woman told me. But at the hospital I found out everything was broken—my teeth. "That was one hell of a fall," the doctor said. "From a great, great height."

—————

The hard, white, straight road shot over the Forked Deer and Big Sandy rivers. Shadow patches drove among the traffic.

As though escorting me, a highway patrolman in dark glasses rode same speed to my left. His cruiser was cream colored; its top, marine blue.

Now it rained and I snapped on the windshield wipers. With their first thwack they made a snarl. They had a load of mud and wet debris to haul.

The cop tooped his horn at me and zoomed out of sight.

The storm changed the sky, left it whirling and wild, left an eerie warmth and the air current electrified. Insects worked a steady zipper sound. The horizon looked Dutch, demented as a Ruisdael.

"Hot Thing" and "Parachute Woman" bammed on the radio.

For something to think, I pretended I was an East Berlin reporter, here in the States to report. "So the file I send back will run in three aligned columns, each beginning with the same sentence fragment—some flexible line with a lot of application—and then the line will echo in each column's final phrase or maybe only in the last word."

The car tires' chant on the pavement was all vowel sounds, tonal now and close below.

"This is a good project," I told myself. I said, "Or at least it kills the miles."

I noticed a fence around a satellite dish when I dashed open the rubber draperies of my motel room in Memphis.

A movie floated around out there and I meant to snag

it and let it roll on the TV if it wasn't an Elvis. I thought I could probably look at almost anything else.

Although not a film about infidelity, or one with cops committing back-country killings. I didn't want to see a movie with a swamp in it. Or one with evangelist char-acters. Not a western. Nothing with Charlton Heston, nor a hurricane; nor a movie about a flood.

Raf had installed the car with surround-sound stereo. As I drove the tunnel and bridge sequence across the Ohio, I listened to a Chinese violinist playing Debussy.

It was dawn. Barges rode the river. Above them, gulls made geyser shapes.

I imagined Mario, my father, riding with me; having a good time, chiding Debussy for political colorlessness.

I cleared the city and got a view of the flat foresty distance ahead. The landscape had left in it some of the burn of late autumn.

The car's suspension seemed brilliant. The speed bumps I rumbled over in the lot for a hardware store were no more than muffled ripples.

I bought gardeners' gloves at the hardware, and from their vending machines I got a cinnamon doughnut and a cardboard cup of coffee. I ate the doughnut, took whis-pering sips from the cup, which I held in the floppy fingers of the gigantic gloves.

The sky went hectic with snow as I untangled from the turnpike loop in Pennsylvania. The snow was carried on gusts of wind that pushed and pressed on the car.

Under my anorak's sleeves, four cuffs ringed my wrists as I had layered on two more shirts in the washroom of an Octron station.

I crossed over a quiet black river and drove along a ridge of hills with endless pelts of blue spruce, birches, and jack pines.

It was dusk in the iced and glassed Allegheny Range and lights were up in the farmhouses here, but now and then out of the rockface a tree signaled in orange or red.

I veered off 80 and followed some frosted gravel roads through finger-lake and deer country.

Raf's parents lived near here, on the farm where he grew up. "He used to be a tractor," I said aloud. I didn't want to visit the parents. There was too much Raf in Raf's dad's smile.

The northern horizon was sherbet green.

I passed storm-shocked trees that sprayed snow like aerosol, horses picking over the puddled land, barbed-wire fences covered with frizzled ivy, rows of broken brown corn stalks, a silver-capped water tower, a park with a hundred picnic tables turned onto their tops.

The evening sun put an oily finish on the snow. I saw spots when I looked straight at it—yellow, blue, magenta.

I drove by a roller rink with tilted skates for a logo, heaps of cut timber, the twin spikes of winking radio towers, a tidy prop plane on display to the road.

I passed a parched orchard, electric towers shaped like huge party dresses, a cluster of floodlights trained on a gorge, a white bowling alley blinking in the late sun, trees with rusty pine cones, fields of twisted weeds, crowd scenes of cattails.

And tires along the roadside; parts and strips and hunks, and some were whole.

The sky shook loose more snow.

Now I had an idea for a long poem on enantiotropy. Barny, the physicist, had talked about it. He said this is the method for something becoming its own opposite, which it does because of a critical pressure, usually; becomes the reverse of what it was or ever intended to be.

My car was hydroplaning. For a weightless moment it went airborne. The steering wheel lost command.

Now the radio speakers yelped as the car let down. I'd been narrating the episode, I realized; for no one, carefully detailing it aloud.

I guided off after a FOOD-PHONE-GAS sign.

An eighteen-wheeler, also exiting, raised rooster tails of slush that boomed onto my windshield. When my wiper blades stroked the water away, fixed ahead was a funny melting world: a building like a stone hunting lodge, people, dozens of squat and stout fuel pumps.

I was shuffling boot to boot inside a souvenir shop holding a cold phone receiver that smelled of lipstick and hairspray. I had it in mind to call my mom to tell her about the postcard and that Raf was or had been there in Wasnascawa.

"Shame, shame," I was saying now, seated on a bent leg on the floor. I was in the position of a schoolyard marble shooter. My left palm stung. I studied the corrugated tread on my boot. Some people were watching me watch the boot.

"Oops," a man said. "Still in one piece?"

I saw my canvas handbag a yard away. "What happened to me?" I asked.

"We don't know," said one of the watchers.

"I fell? I've never done that. I've never fallen down and not *known* it. I don't remember falling."

My left leg hurt, hip socket to knee joint.

"Thank you," I told whoever was helping me. "So crazy."

A black man was helping me. His face was shaped like a pear. His cheeks bulged; his bald forehead was narrow. He wore a Dickie's shirt and chinos.

When I bent to scoop up my handbag he held me by the elbow.

"Well, that could mean something," he said, "that falling down."

"I know what it means," said one of the watchers.

"You're wrong. Go fuck!" I yelled, and the four or five of them rushed away.

"Come on, little chicken," the black man said. He led me to dining tables—a cafeteria. Above the frying vats was a mural—a battle scene from the Revolutionary War.

I limped. "Who are you?" I asked the man.

"You better sit down," he said.

"Why? Are you calling the police?" I didn't sit down.

"No, just wait here. Name's Richard," he said.

I kept my gaze on the napkin dispenser and slid onto a chair before an orange tabletop. I looked at the paper napkins until the Richard man returned. He brought a mug of tea with a saucer clapped over it.

"All for you, now listen up," he said.

"My father says, 'Listen up,' " I said. "Mario, my father. He says it all the time."

"I'm no advice giver. I don't call police. I just say what *I* would do. I'd drink your tea. Then I'd take the cot room we have. We have a room with cots. I'd watch a little TV, and then I'd get some sleep."

"I'm drinking it," I said. I fixed a stare on the Revolutionary War mural, at its purple streaks of trees, its redcoats, muskets, cannons. I drank my tea.

From outside, the turnpike traffic sounded like saw blades and knives being sharpened.

Through the window I saw squiggly trees, and the light—a misty fluorescent pink now.

"Just one of those things," the Richard man was saying. "Only I'd be smart about it." He repeated: "I don't give advice or call the authorities. But if I were stoned, or I fell down in public and couldn't remember it, I wouldn't be ashamed. I wouldn't apologize. I wouldn't feel guilty just yet."

"May I leave?"

"It would be foolish," he said.

"I want to go," I said. "I'm going."

At the next motel, in the vending area, I saw a figure in the shadows under the stairs. "What're you doing back there?" I asked.

"Nothin'. My quarter rolled."

A man drifted into the light and stood on the rug runner before the plump red soda machine.

"I'm a guest here," he said.

The man was a salesman. He wore a Sigma Chi ring, a

wedding band, and a ring etched with baseball bats—an American League champ ring.

His suit was uniform blue, and his loosened tie was shiny. He looked overfed.

"You thought I was somebody you knew? Who? Do I look like somebody? Your husband?"

"No, actually not at all. Although, who knows? I haven't seen him in a while," I said.

"Tell *me* about divorce," said the salesman. "I been on the other end, of course."

I was thinking this man had been handsome and agile once, but now he was neither of those and he didn't know it. He stood with his wide shoes set far apart.

I dripped change into the soda machine.

"Some cases," the salesman said, "it's divorce. Mine, it was burglary. It was hit the road, Jack, and don't even take your p.j.'s. I had to start over at thirty-one, with nothing. Meantime, she's doing the town. I know *all* women aren't that way, but I didn't for a while. She's got every barkeep in every bar in Hagerstown knowing her by name—and I mean *first* name."

"No longer bitter?" I said.

My pink can of soda chunked down into the PULL HERE bin.

"Everybody says it, but it's my kid I feel worst about. Maybe he don't need a father, but he's got *that* for a mother."

"What'll you have?" I said.

"You're buying? In that case, root beer."

"How long you been here?" the salesman asked. He sat on the corner of my bed.

"Only an hour or so."

"You get lonely on the road," he said. "Get a load of me. Did that sound like a come-on or what? 'You get lonely on the road. . . .' "

He had a strong jaw and his hair was neatly combed. People had perhaps told this man he looked like a hefty young version of Dan Rather.

"Were you an outfielder?" I asked him.

"My ring," he said and glanced at it. "Naw, shortstop. Batted—damn, I almost forgot. Fifth, actually." He was grinning and trying not to. "Are you a fan?"

"No," I said. "My husband was, a little."

"He's where?" the salesman asked.

I shrugged and didn't answer.

He said, "All I meant was *I* get lonesome on the road, so I go into these ladies' rooms. . . ." He shook his head. "I wind up *talking* to a woman in her room. It doesn't mean anything. The truth is, I'm still very tight with my ex-wife."

"That's good," I said. "I had a reason for inviting you in, but it wasn't sex."

He seemed confused. "It wasn't? Or not right away, you mean. Not yet, you're saying."

"Not ever at all. I wanted you to listen to something. I could read it, and then you could tell me whether or not your attention starts to flag."

"All right, sure," the salesman said.

I opened my laptop machine and brought the long poem up on the screen.

I said, "Just let me know if your mind wanders, O.K.?"

The salesman waved his hand after thirty seconds. "Stop. Start again, slower," he said. "That first part was really long."

" 'Enantiotropy,' " I read, and reread the first stanza.

"Boy oh boy," said the salesman.

"Do you still want to listen, or should I just quit?" I asked.

"I'm listening. . . ."

I read all sixteen pages of the poem.

"You *wrote* that? That's all *yours*?" he said. "It's science? Or social science? What would you classify it?"

"Well, it's a poem now, is all."

He said, "I get *that*. Yeah. Which I *liked*. I liked it a lot but . . ."

"What? Go ahead and tell me."

"I liked the poetical writing," he said.

"Never mind, fine. You don't need to say anything else. What's your name again?" I asked.

"Jeff."

"Jeff. Great. I only wanted for someone to listen. Now I see it could be better. That it still needs tinkering."

"O.K., but can I ask you something?" he said. "Why'd you write that? Did somebody make you, or assign it to you, or what?"

"No, I just got interested in the idea."

During my reading, Jeff had stripped off his jacket. His thick waist had lifted the tube of his vest. His shoulders were wide, though; his biceps hard with muscle.

"Did you do free weights? My husband again. He did them for a while."

"Believe me," Jeff said, "I have *done* free weights. I'm in one-seventy, you wanna talk more or anything. We could go to dinner. You know, we *ought* to. I'm on an account."

"Good, because I'm not, and these motel stops are breaking me."

"So let's do. One-seventy," he said again.

———

I hiked a mile along the mud ridges behind the motel after I spoke to Raymond.

"Good, good, this is good, *talk* to him," Pru had said and surrendered the phone.

"Paige," Raymond said—just my name.

"Hi, I finally got you. I wanted to say I'm sorry for the way I left."

"Case of this time *she* does the leavin'."

"Oh, please don't think that, Raymond. Remember how you said Raf's just ashamed and confused? That he's not running from me? Well, I'm *all* of those, and scared."

"Of?"

"Not sure . . ."

"That was horseshit about Raf," Raymond said. "You left *the next morning*. Couldn't of thrown a dart straighter at the bull's-eye. You were runnin' from me."

I thought about saying I was running after Raf; telling Raymond I'd got the postcard. But running after, running from—neither was true and both were.

I stood in some glacial valley now. There were rock-mean mountains all around and, crowding down on them, the white northern sky.

A boy loitered by the door of my room when I got back. His hair was fluffy, shoulder length. His clothes were weathered blues. He puffed on a cigarette; flicked it. The heel of his engineer's boot was braced on my car's fender.

"You own this?" he asked.

"I'm the driver . . ."

"Same thing to me," the boy said.

Now he sat where Jeff had, on the bed, and smoked a Marlboro. He said, "I've trashed some motel rooms in my day."

"You're just out of high school, right? I bet you like heavy metal bands. You've probably *been* in bands. And you like getting high, but you don't do coke."

"No, I don't do coke," the boy said. "Everything else you said is wrong."

"You drink a lot of beer, I would guess; and have smoked great amounts of reefer *in your day*."

"I've got reefer. Beer makes me yak. I'd rather have liquor than either one of 'em," the boy said, fidgeting with a threaded bracelet on his wrist.

I said, "Your girlfriend dresses you."

"She'll maybe pick out a shirt or something."

"Your dad's, hmm, a franchiser? And recently divorced from your mom. You still sort of live with her, only she's been dating a man you hate so you hardly ever go home except for meals and to do your laundry."

"Wrong, wrong, wrong," the boy said.

"Your grades were pretty low and you almost didn't graduate. So you're thinking vocational school, trade school."

"My father fuckin' owns this town," he said.

I said, "He works, and you see him once a month."

"Yeah, you know everything," said the boy. His lean grin tried to take away some of the flush rising up like a slap mark on his neck. "You know *you* invited me in here."

"You're right, I'm sorry. And the reason was—believe it or not—I wrote a poem I want to read to you."

"Get out," the boy said.

"No, it's really true."

" 'Kay," he said. "Then what happens?"

I shrugged. "I don't have any liquor. And I'm almost broke. It's Saturday. We could smoke your reefer and watch cartoons."

———

The wall was a blazing persimmon. The TV was yelling; Jeff was yelling, and trying to look past me into the room. He kept asking, "*Is that your son?*"

I was cocooned in the bed's comforter, wearing it like a cape. "It's TV!" I said to Jeff. "We're just watching TV!"

"Are you in trouble here? Tell me. You can tell me, I'm a cop."

"A cop? You are not. You're a salesman. You were born one, you can't get out of it."

"No," he said, "I'm really a police officer. Whoever told you I was a salesman?"

"You were a shortstop, now you're a salesman, remember?"

"I *was* a shortstop fifteen *years* ago and that was only . . . no shit, what's going on here?"

Jeff swung the door open and looked around the room, "What is going on?" he asked the boy. "I'm the police. I came by to take this woman to dinner."

To me, Jeff said, "O.K., skip dinner. I'll leave you alone with this. But cool it on the TV volume or you'll get yourself tossed out."

"You really the heat?" the boy asked him.

"Not really really," I said.

"I come by to take you to dinner, I find Sodom and Gomorrah," Jeff said. "Well, cops can party too, babe."

"Babe?"

He said, "I'll be in room one-seventy, you need me."

I dreamt a disembodied hand touched my breast. I dreamt I was driving the Buffalo Speedway. I dreamt I fell down and hurt my leg, and Raymond's dog, Connie, was woofing.

Jeff ate a sausage wound in dough. He tasted his coffee, dabbed his mouth with a paper napkin.

His tie was noosed high on his thick throat. He had his vest buttoned. His dark hair lay flat and wet from his morning shower. He wore a bristling camel's-hair topcoat.

"Crow-suns," he said. "They got ham, sausage, egg or no egg. I like the sausage. It's embarrassing but I *like* road food. You sure look like holy hell, Paige. Holy hell itself."

It was early morning. I had a paper cup of orange juice before me that I hadn't touched. I'd checked out and followed Jeff in his Celica back to 95. We drove thirty miles to this exit with the breakfast Burger King.

"That was a kid you were with. I can't see that. A boy, not a man. Yeck," Jeff said.

"*With?*" I said. "Why argue?"

After a bit, he said, "I mean, if last night was any sample, hey, no wonder you lost your husband. I don't make judgments; I'm not the judging kind. But that was a bad scene—pot, I could smell it. A kid. Not like I haven't *heard* of such stuff but don't you go to church?"

I looked at him.

"What church do you go to? I want to know. The Black Sabbath Church of Evil Sin?"

"Yes, that one. You've said it all now, Jeff. You can calm down."

"I'm calm. You better eat though, lady. Let me buy you some animal protein."

"No, really, thanks."

"Where are you going, besides east?" he asked me. "I just realized I don't even know."

I said, "I'll follow your car for a while. Then, I suppose, I won't follow it."

"Makes sense," Jeff said.

Against disease in Cameroon, we took Proquanil and Paludrine, Fansidar plus Chloroquine. Mario drank his tea without milk or sugar but with a little salt; the same for fruit juice. We ate no salads, nothing that might've been rinsed in bad water. Bilharzia or hepatitis happened from bathing in the rivers or lakes, but the sea was safe. The first two weeks, every day, we swallowed an antibiotic named Trimethoprimsulphamethoxazole.

BEAT LIKE
A HEART

AS I CROSSED the Rhode Island–Massachusetts border, a string orchestra on the car radio made music for a green, graceful landscape and not what I saw in this horizontal stretch, which seemed optionless and menacing, with clouds that were dirty, industrial, shaped like attacking fish.

I felt forces at work on me, vise grips closing down with each revolution of the earth.

Thumbtacked to the front door of the Brookline place was a puffy manila envelope, sealed and—no postmark or stamp—hand delivered. Inside was a single sheet of paper, ripped from a grocery sack into the ragged profile of some forgotten country.

I stood in the bike clatter and yelp of the neighbor kids, in cold sunlight, and read the pencil writing.

Paige,
They got me this time, or HAD me. The poleeze. Luckily I started wiggling & could not stop as in con-

vulsions and I donut recommend them & even the cops didn't want me like that—shoulda seen it—so I went from the pokey into the bug house or SOMEPLACE like a toilet but with doctors. It's been tough to get to a phone. Withal, now am OUT and back in town, but I got to go away for three days or a week but I'll meet you out at your angel mom's inn on the shore & real soon? Is it Wednesday 2-day. So next Monday I'll see u??? Please? I got the gall to suggest it all because you're the only girl for me, girl

And I thought: You ought to know, Raf. You've tried most of the others.

I felt stupid crying in front of kids on bikes and my Irish neighbor, who was passing with his drugstore copy of the *Globe.*

"You-ah beck?" he asked.

"I'm back," I said after a mighty inhale that gave me some control.

He touched his newspaper to his hat brim, a fine salute.

Inside was dusty, and the bed had been undone and done. An empty Johnnie Walker Black bottle lay among the pillows.

I had to sleep, and so flung off the used linen, flapped down new.

Sleep didn't come. I fetched and lugged back to bed *The Concise History of the World*, and read from Mesopotamia to the Missouri Compromise before my eyes lowered to a close.

———

They opened after a few minutes, and my body jerked up and rolled out of the bed. I couldn't sleep in it alone anymore.

I did laundry, packed clean clothes, went shopping for supplies. I would *live* at the inn, was my thinking; a place that had been good for me. I liked being there; liked Dottie. I *loved* Dottie, although I never had figured out why on earth she left my dad.

Zigzagging up from Reading International to Harvard yard, my knapsack pointy with the spines of new hardbacks, I thought: "Why did I do this to myself? Why didn't I buy detective novels, books a person could *read*?

A student with windburned cheeks recited a sonnet she'd written. Her eyes were wet. Her throat sounded constricted.

This was my class—forms writing—but Johnny Belize had it for the two semesters I was on leave with my arts grant.

The class, a casual seminar, ran itself. Students and Johnny were gathered in the undergraduate lounge. Johnny listened only now and then. He seemed close to dozing in a leather armchair.

When the student finished reciting, the young man seated next to her lifted himself from his chair. He said, "Well, that was fine, Olivia."

"The ending has the wrong effect, though, don't you think?" Olivia said, but with relief in her voice. "Don't you think the final line's cheaty? A piece of exposition? Maybe a correlative would've been better."

"One does speculate—how to say it?—about the *tonal* consequences of unvarying values in that last. And, as you suggested, Olivia, why so much narrative?" asked the young man.

He went on talking that way for a while.

Olivia put pages into her valise and nodded or tipped her head in consideration.

I had come by to check on my student-work drop box —pleasingly empty—and more to say hello to Johnny.

Class broke up. Students stood, gathered notebooks, parkas and gloves, tote bags, satchels.

"War or babies," someone muttered, moving alongside me in the hall. "Those're all Olivia can *write* about."

I visited my vacant office. The young man who'd talked in class appeared and pantomimed knocking on the already open door.

The office was a narrow room, with two walls traveling a slanted ceiling and two others built with bookshelves— almost emptied by borrowers.

The file cabinets were mine, and of the desktop stuff, I owned the stapler and the crane-neck lamp.

Johnny Belize joined us. He was forty or so. He wore his good wool suit, wingtips with leather laces, one of his good silk ties. He had height, lankiness, drowsy eyes, a kindly face.

"How's Raf?" he asked me.

"Missing in action again," I said.

"But of course he is," Johnny said. "Your bottle!" From the hat shelf in the little coat closet, he slid a pinch bottle of Haig & Haig that I kept for visiting parents, poets, faculty. He held the bottle delicately in his fine-boned hands, as if it were an antique.

"You are a lovely crazy man!" the student said to him.

"Hardly," Johnny said. "I'm paranoid and mean. Ask anyone who knows me. Professor Deveaux? Am I not caustic? A moocher? A sot?"

"All of those," I said.

The young man helped himself to the Scotch. He plugged his mouth with the bottle, gulped twice, lowered it, and gasped. He swabbed his lower lip. He said in a rusty, charred voice, "Water, water, water!"

Almost immediately, Johnny was drunk and throwing the paper trash that had remained in my wastebasket out the office window.

He said, "I've finally reached a saturation point with women. But for you, Paige. I know it's momentary, but, lordy, look at your leg!"

"And I have another one," I said.

"I know! But I don't know what to do. Eat them or take pictures or something!"

"Too bad age will soon ravage you," the young man said and followed with a sigh.

When Johnny had thrown out all my trash, he went away and came back toting a filled plastic sack of his own.

"You can't!" the young man said.

"Cambridge is a hole. I'm getting even by filling it," Johnny said.

"How else are you getting even?" asked the young man.

"Look, who are you?" I asked him.

Johnny unloaded his trash sack by holding it out the window, upside down. A newsletter flew. I heard the thunk of a half-eaten apple.

"Surely no one could blame Raf for fleeing," Johnny said as he brushed bits of paper from the sleeves of his suitcoat. "*Anywhere but here.*"

———

That evening I ate in a restaurant in Boston Harbor, aboard a ferry that parked there year round.

There was moonlight. There were thrashing winds batting newspapers and whipping boat-ride ticket bits into squalls.

The sea washing up had a rainbow skin and floated wobbly stripes of reflection from the ferry's lights, the table candles, the moon.

I smashed a tab of butter onto a hot tear of bread in my cupped palm.

The ferry, the drive from Houston, sleeplessness, Raymond, Raf, his letter . . . I was swaying.

The old South Shore hotel where my mom was manager-caretaker was forty minutes from Boston in the least traffic, with another twenty needed to navigate the lanes that wound through Hampham and then the town of Wasnascawa. The roads got skimpier for the world's end village of Cape Head, where stood the Seahorse Inn.

Houses crowded the bayside artery and blocked the rainy wind on the way out of Hampham.

At the tip of Wasnascawa I crossed over to the peninsula's ocean side and went toward the headlands. Here were two miles of naked beach, tidal marsh, acres of boat-parking space.

The surf crested high and white and toppled with a roar that was everywhere in the air.

At the inn, I went up a slate walk to a red door with a brass knocker.

"My girl's come a-calling," Dottie said, and we hugged and patted each other. She held me away for study.

Her eyes reddened, so I said, "Your cats are escaping."

"Otto and Spotto," she said. She had given my behind a pretty good pinch.

She pulled me into the lobby area, where a lacquered fish arced over the mantel and most of the furniture was shrouded with drop cloths or sheets.

My mom had kept the same look since the forties—mules, sweater sets, long hair rolled back off her forehead.

"She's pinup stuff," Raf had said and sighed after their first meeting.

Spotto scooted across a braided rug into the big kitchen area with Dottie and me casually following.

Making coffee, Dottie used complicated German equipment—bean grinders, valves, tubes, and spigots. "Where is he?" she asked, meaning Raf.

"Seventh or eighth circle of hell," I said.

"Poor guy," said Dottie. She was uncritically crazy about him.

Winter-storm thunder rolled around outside. The cats followed its noise from room to room, window to window.

"Something's boiling out there," she said.

I said, "That goddamn storm has been on my back all the way from Houston. It hates me!"

Dottie tasted her coffee and smiled. "You must have some of this."

"I'm already shaking without it, Mom."

"Then here's what we should do. Go for a ride, smoke some reefer, and I'll tell you some giant news."

Besides being caretaker for the Seahorse, Dottie wrote a column for the Cape Head weekly, *The Pulse*. Hers was a consumer-activist column that'd been picked up by a few other coastal-area papers. "Conscience Shopping," it was called.

Now as we drove away from the inn and into the strange afternoon, she said, "What I've finally learned and have been doing lately is taking a truth, like that some appliance makers have nuclear weapons contracts, air-and-space-weapons contracts. Or parent companies in South Africa, yet! Or most recently I've been writing about toiletries—mouthwash, shampoo, and what-all—emphasizing the importance of who's getting the money and for what. All in a thousand words, until I can think, 'There, I've done my damage.' "

Shopping with her would be hell.

I said, "In fact, he may be on his way here."

"Who?"

"Raf. I'm sorry. I got a letter. . . . He'll probably never show, but he *might* come, soon. Monday, maybe. It's hard for me to think about too much else."

"And me yapping and yapping," Dottie said.

Above the bluffs at land's end was the dying village of Cape Head, balanced on hilly high ground over cliffs that were getting washed away, that fell to the rocky beach. Every time I had looked the cliffs were steeper, closer to the village. One lofty old hotel was already going over in a spill of stones and timber and pieces of plaster walls.

A match scraped. I looked over and saw Dottie bent into the serious business of lighting a marijuana cigarette. The comic novelty of Dottie's getting buzzed had worn off long ago.

She exhaled in a gasp.

The view from the climbing road was of toy boats rocking on the churned-up bay, two winking lighthouses. Wasnascawa, far below us, was a smudge like an ashes and oil-chalk sketch.

"We're on shaky ground," my mom said, holding her breath, her voice strained hoarse.

"So don't hog it, Mom," I said, and Dottie took my remark dead level. She passed me the cigarette.

I steered up a spiraling Cape Head street, coughing myself red from the smoke.

Built into the hillside were an abandoned filling station, the one-room post office; the gambrel-roofed house that was the library; a Catholic church called Our Lady of the Angels; and on top of the land mass where the road dead-ended, a stone watchtower.

I parked there and we looked at the sea and distant sky where there was a flock of snow clouds. A gust of freezing rain splattered away the view.

We drove out of Cape Head village and down between lines of leaf-stripped trees onto the Point Road and out the spur of land where the inn perched.

"I've seen Mario," Dottie said.

"Oh, really? How is he these days?"

"Fine," she said. "He comes up on the train from Providence and we eat somewhere or he just visits with me."

"Wait, stop. *Dad* Mario? I just heard you. You're telling me you've been dating Dad?"

"Seeing him, yes," she said.

Dottie seemed to focus on the cawing gull that paced along beside the car.

I turned up a dirt driveway and went through a gate in the trestle fencing, under the carved sign—THE SEAHORSE INN—swinging wildly from a post.

Ahead, the main house looked both simple and vast, with its steep, low-hipped roof and three chimneys. Annexes and new additions sprawled. Well away stood the Dutch barn that Dottie used for a garage.

"Are you taking him back?" I asked her, but she was gaping lovingly at the inn.

She said, "Privacy."

The dirt drive had potholes and puddles. I charged instead up the sodded hay-blond lawn, past the weather-blackened monumental anchor stuck there. The yard was frozen mineral hard.

We went into the inn through a delivery entrance, into the taproom, where the floor was uneven, a pegged wood. There were ash ceiling beams, and a walk-in fireplace, its mantel blackened from smoke.

It was Friday afternoon, so I faced three days of waiting for Raf, but the Seahorse made the best site for a waiting ordeal.

"Tote in your luggage. I'll fix us drinks," my mother said.

"This is all of it," I said, meaning the long duffel strapped over my shoulder.

On the mantel lay a gathering of seashells—sundials, jewel-box shells, great lilac volutes. Beside them was a talking radio.

From the radio, a woman broadcaster predicted gale-force winds and snow tomorrow, with a disaster snow blizzard on Sunday; possibly a foot of snow.

"Let it come!" Dottie said.

We ducked under a blockhouse door and crossed the front lobby, where Dottie bopped the bell on the registry desk. The chime brought Fredo, the freckled dog, writhing and leaping in greeting.

"Say hello but be a nice chap," Mom told him. "We're baked."

We came to the saloon. She stepped behind the bar and toe-tapped a floor switch that ignited yellow lights—spots trained on a shimmering assembly of liquor bottles in back of her.

"You and Mario?" I said.

For now, the storm sounded far away, a reminder of storm.

Mid July, right before Houston, I had driven to Providence to visit my dad. He was out in his garden, tying up tomato plants.

"So thin," I thought.

Mario held a Tootsie Pop in his mouth. I could smell the orange candy.

His face was tanned but his flowing hair had gone foam white. He seemed a few inches shorter. His cheeks had collapsed inward and his eyebrows were bushy.

He cracked the lollipop and finished it, poked the white cardboard stick into the ground of his garden.

Monteverdi blew from the kitchen. So did the odors of rosemary and wine.

A cool twilight was settling down the ribbed hill from Mario's, and the city in the light glowed lavender.

After kissing me, my dad said, "See da garden? It's not for me, it's for the groundhogs, the rabbits. This is the thing I'm supposed to mind. I plow, plant, weed, spread manure, bone marrow. The food comes up. It's good food. The animals is hungry, they eat it. They're hungry so they do. I'm supposed to mind and blow out their brains or poison them? Oh, listen!"

"I know," I said.

"Lee-la-da-deeee!" Mario sang. "Let them eat, I think. I'm not going to get them for it. Who am I, Elmer Fudd guarding carrots? No-lo-ta-deee! You have good legs, woman."

"Thank you," I said. "But, so, Dad? Why *have* a garden?"

"Endeavor! Exercise! I *buy* my carrots and da vegetables in a grocery store same as you. But now, as to the tomatoes. I care deeply about these tomatoes. So I drive a bargain. Eat the fucking cucumbers, radishes, zucchini. Stuff yourselves and God go with you. But leave the tomatoes for Mario. And they do. They're honorable."

He wore a workshirt and a flower-printed tie, corduroys with deep cuffs.

Patting my bare arm, his hand was callused, hard as a ram's horn.

Under a Dutch elm, the tire swing threw an O shadow on the velvety grass.

"Listen," he said. "It's fine if you come by and my heart is full. Equally fine if you don't. What for? I'm not lonely. How is Raf?"

"Gone," I said. "In Houston, I think. I'm going to try there, anyway. I must be stupid."

"No, don't insult me, Piagga, with you are stupid!"

"All right, all right."

"You know what my dad used to say? At dinnertime? Your Grandfather Amelio?"

"What did he say?"

"He would look up at me and he would say, he would sigh and say, 'Let's eat.' "

Setting my overnight things in Mario's guest room, I had noticed a new mural on the left wall.

In my bedroom in our house in Maryland, Mario had

painted "Apollo's Victory Over the Python" opposite my bed. I was eight or nine. I hadn't wanted ballerinas or circus ponies. Struggle, muscles, and violence were what I asked for.

Mario had shrugged, nodded; primed the plaster wall surface. Later he pencil-sketched a twisting dragon and a descending god, and overnight painted the scene in with thin brushfalls of sienna, brown, and dark brown.

Over dinner that July evening, Mario said, "I'll tell you what about Monteverdi. Opera's turning around, time for a changing point. Monteverdi doesn't get shaked up. Already he did the plays, the madrigal, also ballet. Most of all, he knows music. For *Orfeo*, he has every instrument played by the greatest musicians alive!"

For Mario, opera was history—what people believed and when, their angers and passions.

"Are you working at all?" I asked him.

"Sketches."

"May I see them?"

"No," Mario said, "they're weak."

"I bet they're not weak."

"Not weak," he had said. "They're just not strong."

I sprawled in the inn's fancy sitting room, where sofas upholstered in silk crowded a marble fireplace. An afternoon fire there snapped logs on a tiered piece of ironwork. Persian rugs were squared around. Two floor lamps with parchment shades lighted a magazine in my lap.

"I'm so trashed," Dottie said.

"Me too. In a sense."

"Innocence?" she said.

I had pushed off my shoes, hitched up my cargo jeans so I could warm my socks before the log fire.

"Yes, fried and famished and going for food down on the boardwalk," I said.

"When?" Dottie said. "Earlier in the week?"

"We are very, very high, Mother. If this is what life is like for Raf, I have new admiration for him."

"I know," Dottie said. "I think about that."

I said, "I can hardly make a sentence."

"This decade. Or you mean me?" she asked.

"We need food," I said.

We raided the kitchen, in this case a storehouse, with drum cans of vegetables, soups, cooking stuffs posing on utility shelves, hundreds of wine bottles in rows in wire cages, a meat locker, two freezers, Dottie's personal refrigerator.

We loaded china plates with food: cheese, fruit, two tins of smoked oysters, a knitted rope of French bread, chocolate bars. We had coffee in a burnished silver pot. We layered everything onto a room-service cart and trundled it all back to the sitting room.

"You know, we shouldn't eat this with the brandy on top of your Colombian because we'll get fat at our age."

"*Our* age?" Dottie said. "Our age together is one hundred and two."

I said, "Then who cares?"

"Well, I don't. But what about?" she asked.

"Being a fat one-hundred-and-two-year-old."

"I know," said my mother. "Especially at your age and really fat because of all the reefer you smoke and drink brandy and then you eat."

Fredo, the freckled dog, sat in earnest patience, politely begging. I fed him an oyster. "Poor old dog," I said.

"You know he isn't?" my mom said. "That's son of Fredo; Fredo Two."

"Can't be. Same dog," I said. "I wrote a poem on enantiotropy."

"It hurts me to laugh," said Dottie.

"I wrote in a chorus of parents who were children, anti-fathers and anti-mothers. They admitted, yes, they had been parents, but no, it didn't count."

"The Fredo you remember *was* really old and a beach-ball, a tubbo," Dottie said.

I rolled down my pants' cuffs and positioned my feet back in my shoes. "If we get snowed in here, I just pray Raf can make it."

The fireplace log burned through and slumped suddenly, thumped, releasing a swarming spiral of red sparks.

"My heart!" Dottie said.

"Eat a pear," I said.

I told her the little port city in Cameroon where Mario and I had stayed couldn't be found on maps, that the only way in was to ferry down from Calabar. I said that the Mermoz, one of our hotels, had a beer machine, and that each night the guests would get drunk and sing, "I go backwards ever; forwards, never."

"So what?" Dottie said. She had cleared a space on a writing table with her forearm and dropped her head. An afghan made a drape tent over her.

The telephone out at the registry desk jangled.

"Who am I?" I said to the caller. "Who are you?"

I yelled to my mom, "Someone named Paul?"

"Say hi and sorry but I'm too tired to talk right now," she said.

"Dottie's wasted," I told him.

———

Down in Wasnascawa, there was still light but it was burning out fast by four that afternoon. Blizzard-driven, the surf came against the sea wall with crashes that spattered down into a smaller noise, like applause for home runs at some distant stadium.

Ice had shellacked the boardwalk under me, so for traction I made each step a stomp. There was a paste-white fog. The wind beat my hair forward, gave me blinders on both sides.

I shoved into a year-round bar called the Ocarina.

The best booths were in back. My favorite had a team photograph of the Cape Head Women's Softball Club, 1986 South Shore Park League Champions. Third one in, on a bench, sunburned and smiling, was Dottie.

The customers today were three Coast Guard wives, a town selectman, and the lobstermen regulars.

I sat under a fight poster for Marvelous Marvin Hagler who used to train out around the beach.

"Hey, Paige," the waitress said. "Where's Raf?" Her name was Connie Del Verona. She had a waist-length red hair braid and black-lacquered nails.

"He's around. Espresso," I said.

One of the all-day drinkers sauntered over. Dick was his name. Looking very disheartened, he scooted beside me in the booth.

"Hey, Paige. Where's Raf?" he said.

I remembered Dick ran a day trawler out of Kitahassett for a living.

"How's the fishing?"

"Another week of this storm shit and I go under. So is Raf in town? I love that sucker."

"Hiding out, you know?"

Dick liked hearing that. He grinned.

"I love that sucker," he said again. He wore yellow

rubber overalls and a matching parka that reeked of the sea and booze. His streaming beard and hair seemed to pull his eyes and mouth down as if he were melting in his misfortune. He was a nightmare version of Raf.

"We tried goin' out yesterday, to the *shelf*, believe it or not. You want some of this?" Dick said, offering me his brimming doubles glass. In his raw-knuckled grip the glass shook.

"I came here to get straight," I said.

"You came to a bar to get sober?"

That was true. I came for the cold air, the walk, to escape the temptations of the inn; came because Raf and I had had some jolly times in these booths.

Dick guzzled his red whiskey and shivered.

He rasped at me, "You do writing, don't you?"

"No, just poetry," I said.

"Right, well, here's a poem you can write. This's what God told me last time we were chatting," Dick said. Hunching closer and taking my wrist in his hand, he said, "Fornicate and be fruitful." He unrolled his long tongue and panted at me.

I said, "Oh, Charlie?"

Nervous Charlie owned the place. He ran the Ocarina's grills and tended bar. He was bouncer too, and with his darting maroon eyes, missed nothing. He never went far from the cash register, where his baseball bat was stashed.

"Charlie's getting the Louisville Slugger," I said to Dick.

"Raf's wife, and she throws this kinda crap at me. Gets Charlie angry. Raf's a close buddy of mine."

"Then let go of my wrist, Dick, and keep your tongue in your mouth."

Charlie had moved our way and he carried the tape-handled bat. "You two all right? Where's your husband, Paige?" he asked me.

"Running for governor," I said.

"All that's happened was I got a little lippy, Charles," Dick said. He looked bad.

"You gonna be sick now, Dick?" Charlie asked.

"How would I know?" Dick said. "Funny kind of day I'm having with everything shitting on me." He got up and hobbled away.

Charlie took his ball bat and tucked it under his arm. He leaned against the wall across from me and gave me his sternest look.

The wind pressed hard now on the Ocarina's wet front window. The window had patches of frost.

Charlie's cheek quivered and he said, "In case you haven't heard, things are going awfully rough for the watermen these days. *There's* an injustice to tell about, you and your mother want to write something."

"I'll do it, Charlie. I'll write a septet or a villanelle about fishermen injustice."

"See it when I believe it," Charlie said.

THE SNOW

I DREAMT that Raf lay in the next room, gasping and laughing. His laugh was wheezy but agreeable, and sometimes it degenerated into a shallow cough.

That was true to life, that cough.

Dottie kept the inn's private dining room heated and that's where she found me this morning. She sat across the table, seeming dazed in the light from the new snow.

"You look familiar," she said to me.

I sighed, flicked my computer screen clean. I had been typing shakily, working some lines and words around toward a nonce-rhyme poem.

The freckled dog Fredo loped into the room, yawning as he came.

My mom made a loose fist and dangled her hand in front of the dog's face. "This is the froggy that will hypnotize you," she chanted. She put her nose to the dog's nose, stared into its dogface. Fredo's facial markings gave him an expression of crazed good cheer, as if he found Dottie hilarious, her every action a howl.

I said, "You slept fifteen hours and, having arisen, you smoked dope. Haven't you heard of the war on drugs?"

"This is the normal me," she said. "You just need coffee. I'll make us some, you play with Fredo."

"Mom, I'm writing and he noses me."

To Fredo, she said, "Do you hear this? Go *nose* her. What a bitch!"

Not a gull, but some shifting thing in flight slashed past the window. I watched it kite over the south annex and the layers of outside terraces. The flying thing was a black sheet—a rain poncho, maybe. The wind forced most of it under the house soffit.

I typed some bird names I had memorized because the black shape gave me a chill. "Hooded Merganser. Fulvous Whistling Duck."

Gradually the sheet whirled itself loose. It went witch-like, spinning in a crosscurrent, up, and wrapped itself around the weathercock on the Dutch barn. It stuck there, speared by the pointing metal of the vane.

I gave up on writing for the day, Saturday, and hiked off my hangover, going to the village and back.

Dottie enlisted my help with some upkeep chores. We waxed the nice wooden floors, broomed and dusted the rooms that were still heated and in use. But even by nine that night neither of us could face food. I volunteered to walk Fredo.

"Wear layers," Dottie said.

Behind the inn were white-timber terraces, where the

summer guests would drink and dine. From the terraces, a path with a pipe handrail curled down the bluffs to the beach.

Fredo lunged ahead down the path so that, clenching his leash in my fist, I descended in a barely controlled scuttling fall. In my free mitten was an eight-volt box flashlight.

There was moonlight but scraps of snow clouds were dark, shadowing the beach. The dog paused at an old ice patch to squirt lines of urine. The light at the end of the jetty and the St. Michael's Island light had come on. They twitched like faltering stars.

Fredo hobbyhorsed through a dense clutch of grass, spiky with ice, at the foot of the palisades. Down here the Atlantic winds had scraped away the snow piles, and the beach itself made a kind of flat avenue.

There was an access lane that curved off the Point Road and swerved down a quarter mile to dead end on the beach. Parked at the dead end was an old school bus, I could see. The bus was painted matte black. Beside it were the flames of a campfire.

I headed that way.

"That's deceased," I told Fredo, who was sniffing and whimpering over the big shell of a horseshoe crab.

We walked on, in the direction of the bus. Eerie things lay all along here. I saw a broken eyeless eel, phosphorescent with frost; a rope-soled shoe pointing inland; a dead gull whose white body made a W-shape on the sand.

I got within shouting range of the bus. There were three or four figures idling around the campfire. In its light, they were genderless, mammoth-sized and strange.

Fredo loped ahead; a ridge of fur pricked up along his spine.

The figures had turned to watch.

I waved, tugged on Fredo's leash. He walked low, gargling threats, half dragging me.

A girl broke from the group and headed for me. I could make out her shape and the angles of her face. She carried a stick she pointed. Its strip of shadow pointed too.

"What's going on?" I asked her.

"I dunno—nothing," the girl said.

As we spoke our words vaporized in the warm currents of our breath, froze and blew off.

The girl was scaled larger than I but was only eighteen or twenty, I guessed. "I see you're walking that little dog," she said.

She wore pieces of military garb. The clothes had been bleached and dye-soaked, and in the flashbeam I could see the colors were uneven, streaked and blotched with whites and grays.

She drew scribbles with her branch stick in the damp sand.

I said, "Why are you here? Are you having a party or something?"

Both of us looked around at the bus. There was light inside, and behind green window curtains, plenty of movement.

"He's a cute dog," the girl said. "What's he laughing at?"

"I wondered about your bus, though," I said. "Because this is a private beach, the property where you're parked, see."

She lifted her eyebrows at me, gave a shrug. "It wasn't my idea. We parked on the street earlier but they said we were in the way because of snowplows needing to get through," the girl said.

"Yeah, but when the tide comes in soon, this'll all be underwater."

"That'd be weird," she said.

I aimed my flashlight at the ground. In the beam that came up, the girl's face floated white and serene.

"It's fine with me if you hang around, but the cops could grab you. The Cape Head cops or the MDC cruise past all the time."

"You should tell these fish that wash up, 'Don't rot on the beach because it's private.' "

I said, "I'm trying to help you. We're due for another foot of snow."

The other two from the campfire, boys who were teen-agers or not much older, came over. They wore the same military-surplus clothing.

The taller of the two had on a beret. "Good to see you. Didn't we already speak with you?" he said. He asked his mate, "Didn't we already speak with this person? Dozens and dozens of times?"

"She isn't mad at us. She just says because the beach is private," the girl said.

"Aha," said the second young man.

"She told me the tide's gonna cover up the bus," the girl said.

The whole beach lunged. I felt as though I'd stepped onto an ice floe. I moved backward for balance. The snow clouds had cleared away from the full moon for a second and the clouds' shadows streamed around us.

The girl whipped her stick left and right in the sand.

The beret kid's eyes sparked.

"You should get to high ground," I said.

In the moon's blaze, I felt weightless.

I had to push my way back through a charged and prickling wind. My eyes stung, and there was ticking all around.

When I shot the flashlight's beam I saw a heavy snowfall unfurling in the light cone.

Dottie stood with the door of her big refrigerator spread. She jolted a little when she looked up at me.

I was covered with ice and crystalline snow. I still grasped the flashlight, was still winded from the stair climb.

"Are you O.K.?" Dottie asked.

"No. Crisped. Frightened."

"I'm scared of Alzheimer's," Dottie said. "I'm afraid it's encroaching. I'm pretty certain it is. I read the symptoms and I've got them."

"Oh, fish sticks. What you've had is too much Colombian," I said.

"One detail it took me a long minute to remember one night, and I tell you it had me in chills, was my bank's name, the *name*."

I told my mother, "There are kids on the beach. Well, older than kids—a guerrilla army."

"More power to 'em," Dottie said. She bit the dainty wing of a Cornish hen. "Wherever land ends, you get people, Paige. They'll come. It's saline sympathy."

"This bunch came in a black bus and has sort of uniforms. Any sort of uniform, I get nervous," I said.

Dottie twisted a tiny drumstick from the hen. "I raised you well," she said.

I slept for short intervals, and the all-night classical station interrupted Verdi's *Requiem* on the quarter hour to report that snow was building, roads would be impassable, most churches were canceling tomorrow's services; all should prepare for power outages; the New York Thruway and

New Jersey Turnpike were sealed, the state of Maine had closed; snow would continue falling.

The chance of seeing Raf got further from me with each report.

The bus people invaded one dream that had just started to form. They were chasing Fredo and calling his name. I woke up to the bells from Our Lady of the Angels and an air-raid siren and the groan of the Misery Island fog-horn.

At my window I saw a remade and padded world. Hip-high snow beds winked like sugar through the fog. The Point Road made a barely visible indentation.

Dottie hummed as she coasted around in her suite, the Commodore, straightening and tucking.

"Ready for another day? This one could be serious," she told me.

"That's all I've been hearing," I said.

"The Patriots have the Jets at home. Could mean the play-offs," she said.

"You mean *football*? Mom, we'll be lucky if we keep the power on. And meanwhile, trespassers are freezing to death on the property."

"Look," Dottie said, nodding at the portable TV on the tabletop. A Ninja movie glowed on the teeny screen.

"Kwii-chee-boo-die!" she said and kicked at her reading chair's ottoman. She backhanded a brush from her vanity table; sent it flying a good ten feet.

"Not that the beach is anyone's defined property . . ." I began.

"I'll define the property with my kwoo-chung-chee-boo," Dottie said. She stuck out a thin arm with her fist clenched.

———

I went hiking on the only flat land, the beach, followed it almost to the fork to Hampham. I saw a lot of damage. The boat shack above the Coast Guard station had blown down. The Boston ferry boat had crashed away a huge part of Nathan's Pier.

Far out, the sea was dark, but jade closer in, in the icy shallows. Waves were frozen, as in some monumental sculpture: scalloped white glazed lace.

There were no people, no black bus, only birds picking around the remains of the campsite. And more snow sifting down.

When I was near to the inn, I saw a man in a thin jacket balanced up on a dune. He was shouting at me with his bare hands propped around his mouth for projection.

"Hey, Nanook!" I heard. "Hey! I can't believe it!"

The context was so wrong and weird that it took me six long seconds before I recognized Raymond.

He jogged down the dune and grabbed me, lifted me, twirled me half around. In this pale landscape, he looked Technicolor, with his still-brown face and rope-blond hair. His eyes too seemed different—sapphire blue—out here in the white and gray.

"You look wonderful!" I blurted.

"Well, thank you, Paige. But I never been so fuckin' cold ever. *Ever.* I am dying."

I dragged him at a trot toward the path up the bluffs to the Seahorse.

"Pru sort of reverted in little ways and big ones to who she was before, and I did too, after you escaped, and I just one night was loco and she says to me, 'We got real problems, Ray,' and I said, 'No we don't, none,' and put myself in the beaner-mobile and hit the road."

He ate a chunk of corn bread and swallowed some espresso Dottie had brewed for us.

"Me and the car made it to Newington, Mass., it's called, where the car caught a flu bug and died."

Dottie, who was listening with me, said, "Oh . . ."

"So I was stuck there five hours, in a doughnut place, when this black bus pulls on in with this rock band."

"You know, I was . . ." I said.

Raymond said, "So's I asked the driver where they were bound and he says, 'Boston,' and I say, 'Where?' and he says, 'Where *you* going?' And I'm like, 'Well, in fact, Cape Head,' so he tells me, 'Fine. That's where we'll go!' "

Raymond tossed up his hands. "And then I'm thinkin' this is *not* the world's most successful rock band."

I said, "You know, I was . . ."

"And then last night I'm sleeping in the bus, 'cause the driver can't find this place and we're lost, and it's the first sleep in three days, and real cold, and they give me clothes and shit for blankets, but I'm sleeping, but it turns out later that *you, Paige, are standing outside the bus* telling 'em how they're gonna drown!"

"I've been trying to get that in," I said.

Dottie said, "Well, you made it, you're safe now."

"Goddamn, I'll say," Raymond said.

Up from the dining table and standing behind Raymond, Dottie caught me with a look and mouthed: "Wow!" and "Is he cute!"

"So you had John Donne with his sonnets that he called divine meditations. Probably because he lifted the idea from Loyola, who made up a three-part meditation for his Jesuits. In Loyola's, each part inspired something—memory, empathy, resolve. A combination prayer and workout for the imagination."

"Whoa, stop the speedboat, man overboard," Raymond said.

I apologized. "I'm a little nervous," I said.

"I am not un-nervous, darlin'," Raymond said. "But at least I'm comfortable at last."

I had come in here to deliver a food tray for Raymond. He lay under three quilts on the Shaker four-poster Dottie bought from an auction house in Pennsylvania. This was usually my suite, in fact; the only heated bedroom in the inn besides Dottie's

"It's what time?" he asked me.

"Two. You slept about three hours."

"And I'm ready to hunt bear," he said. "This is ideal."

"Except, Raymond? Raf's due tomorrow."

Raymond looked at the food tray on his lap. Because he didn't touch it, didn't even seem to see it, I knew he was mining a pretty deep shaft of thought.

"You got to quit believing that's ever gonna work, Paige. You and Raf."

"Why? Do you know something I don't? Tell me what!"

"Most people," Raymond said, "finally, they come to simple dreams, you know? Of getting money, or building a good house, or land, or a kid growing up great. They gotta leave behind the ones where they're famous—like a hero jock or movie star—and see that the world'll never know who they are or that they even *lived*. It's a bad moment, havin' to swallow that one. Especially for such big strategists as Raf and me, 'cause we were gonna make films, and act in 'em, and write books, fuckin' you name it."

I said, "But that bad moment passes."

"For some. For Raf, it never. And he's got you around, with your poetry you publish, reminding him. He can't afford to be happy with you. That'd be caving in."

"I'm a *minor* artist, a *footnote* in modern poetry."

"Maybe. But you still might crank up some day and do a killer. You got that chance. Could happen any time, and then somebody in two hundred years might be readin' your poems when the rest of us are just dust blowin'."

"This is such baloney. Five billion people on the planet and my poetry doesn't count any more than stuff Raf's done or you've done. The buildings you two have worked on have steel girders. They'll *be* here."

"We worked on 'em, but we didn't fuckin' *make* them. That's the difference. And Raf does his best work in the air, you may've noticed—talking his talk."

"It's not my fault that he drinks, Raymond, if that's what you're implying."

"No, but how could he be around you and *not* wanna drink? And it'll stay that way until he finds something better than popping bottles and girls and tracking after the mayor's daughter. What's this in this bowl? Looks like cat chow."

"Ah, lemme remember. Dottie said it's chopped mission figs and oat bran. Very healthful. Dottie digs you."

"I can hold off urinating till after I eat," Raymond said. He got the breakfast tray positioned, shook open his napkin. "I'm sorry I made the speech at you and I'm even sorrier that I think it's true," he said.

I pulled a peacoat on over two sweaters and went out the main entrance. Some of the front lawn had been leveled by the wind. It was still snowing. Grass patches showed.

I paused under four stunned birch trees, listening to the far-off whizzing noise of car tires on ice.

From the hoop gate, I saw the stuck car—crunched nose first into a scoop of snow—down on the Point Road before the climb.

"Raf," I thought.

The inn stood on such high ground and in such hard wind that the driveway had been blown nearly clear.

I went snow-blinded into the cold Dutch barn and started up the smoke-colored car. It *always* started.

On the Point Road, I faced the stuck car—a long Granada. Its engine noise was no more than a sewing machine's. Only two of the pistons were firing, I guessed, and those pretty meekly. Thin twists of exhaust spun away.

The Granada's driver got out into the light.

"Where were you trying to go?" I asked from my rolled-down window.

"Lost," the man said.

"I'll tell you, your car's blocking the only way in or out. You *have* to *move*. Any ideas?" I asked him.

"Sure, but not about getting the car going," he said. "More about blowing it up with a stick of dynamite if I had one."

He was thick-waisted, thick-necked, with a ski cap tugged down to just over his eyes.

"Well, I'll call you a tow," I said. "But I bet they're busy out of their minds, so if nobody comes in a while and you get cold, just come up to that inn behind me."

The man didn't thank me, and he looked so skeptically at the Seahorse I got angry.

"And don't tromp on your gas pedal anymore, it makes things worse," I said.

"How could things be worse?" asked the man.

I backed my car around, drove up to the inn, and telephoned the tow garage. They said no, try again tomorrow.

I told Dottie, in her bathroom, that we'd been blockaded by an ingrate in a Granada.

"Where did you need to go?" she asked. She was brushing shadow on her eyelids, blusher on her cheeks.

"You can tell there's a man in the house," I said, stepping around her.

"What is *wrong* with you, Paige?"

As I opened the medicine cabinet, my reflection swung woozily away. "Raymond," I said. "He came up with something pretty smart, bordering on wise. I hate that."

"You wish he were just a big hunk of beautiful cowboy?"

"Wouldn't that be fucking *enough*?" I said.

By three, the storm had us caught; Dottie had smoked a couple joints and fixed me with a warm brandy-coffee mixture.

Raymond had found the inn's wine stock. He was stewing in a dark corner of the saloon with an unopened bottle in his fist. He raked the wine's label off with a thumbnail, saying, "Now this here's distressing. A huge temptation, altogether. It's not enough I'm corralled with two pretty women. But I got on top of that enough liquor to drown a bull. You, me, and the booze could just get into bed and pull up the covers."

"In fact," I said.

Raymond wore my baggiest sweater, an old blue Norway, with snowflakes and reindeer. Still, the sleeves ended too soon for his wrists.

I said, "I better stay alert, though. This's a killer storm. We're marooned. The Mass. Turnpike's closed. The villagers'll probably be evacuated when their heat and lights go. They've already got choppers lifting out hospital patients."

"I hear you," Raymond said.

The man from the stuck Granada, chilled to rose pink and shivering, came through the front doors. He kept his cap on, still down to his eyes, and inspected the place warily.

"I thought you'd show up sooner or later. There's hot coffee if you want," I said.

"Did you call a tow for me or not?"

"Yes, but they can't come just now. You might have to spend the night and wait until tomorrow. I'm sorry."

"I'm not paying for anything," he said.

Raymond came into the foyer. He said, "Goddamn, it didn't work, Paige. You arranged a blizzard just to get this guy's money but he's too smart for you. Now I'll have to escort him back outside."

The Granada man stiffened as if he believed Raymond on all counts.

"Sit down," I told him. "That's free."

I went into the hotel kitchen to get the mammoth restaurant percolator started. The rock-band girl from the black bus stood there in her drapings of rags.

"Do you mind we came in?" she asked me. "We didn't have anyplace else to go. We were freezing in the bus and 'sides, it's stuck."

"I sort of mind that you *broke* in," I told her. "Where're the rest?"

"Off down that hall," she said, and pointed her stick at the door of a wing with locked guest rooms.

"You should get them and bring them in where it's heated, where there're fireplaces and chairs. Raymond's in the sitting room," I said.

"Raymond?" she said. "Whew, is he hot!"

"I'm just letting you know we have emergency guests," I said over the phone to Candy, at the Cape Head Police Department. The CHPD was one man, a guy named Walt Barber, and Candy Barber, his wife, worked the switchboard.

The rock band and Raymond and the Granada man were in the fancy sitting room, curled up on the puffy couches, lying on the Persian rugs, lined up with their backs to the noisy fireplace.

"Who am *I* talking to?" Candy Barber asked.

"Sorry. It's Dottie's daughter, Paige, at the Seahorse Inn."

"Paige! We went skinny-dipping together one Fourth of July, right? Walt almost had to put your husband in jail, remember?"

"It was a grand day," I said.

Candy's voice got lower, more confidential. "Walt's out there on a Ski-doo."

The rock-band boy with the beret was shadowing me at the registry desk. I looked him a question.

"I gotta piss, I admit," the boy said.

"Should I tell the police that? I'm talking here to the police."

"You could send me to jail," the boy said. "They'll let me piss there, probably."

Dottie came down the spiral staircase from the inn's

second floor. She wore a blue serge dress and a cardigan sweater, mules with cotton ankle socks. Fredo skittered along after her.

"Who are these folks, Paige? Why're you using the desk phone?" When she got close, I smelled her spicy perfume.

"Candy Barber's on the other end," I said.

"Candy Barber from the police? Why's she calling?"

"We're helpless, Paige, tell Dottie," Candy Barber said.

I told my mother. "These're the bus people I met on the beach? They're a rock band, I found out. I just wanted to let Candy know they're here and then she can send the Wasnascawa force if we need them."

"Will not. We can't send help to anyone at present," Candy said on the other end of the phone.

"What do you want, son?" Dottie asked the boy in the beret.

"Gotta piss, ma'am," he said.

We could hear the storm leaning hard on the inn.

I jerked my thumb, directing the boy to the closest washroom.

Candy Barber spoke now as if I worked for her but didn't follow instructions well. "Look, you tell Dot that I'm probably sending over more victims. The shelter's full. We're getting severe power outages. You know, blizzard of seventy-eight out here, people died. You've got the room, heat, hot water, food. . . ."

"You're her mother?" the boy in the beret asked Dottie. "I miss mine."

Fredo arched and stretched, put the tip of his snout on the boy's knee.

"Sweet doggie," the boy said.

"Very sweet," Dottie said, watching as the boy crouched and roughed up Fredo's mane.

"You must be a good son," she said.

The telephone felt lighter in my grip and I realized Candy Barber had hung up on me.

I went through the crowd of guests into the taproom. I squinted out a bubble window—like a porthole on a cruise ship. I saw branches, all gristle and knots, pieces of broken trees flying by. Beyond was the straight edge of ocean-horizon.

"We can feed you and give you tea or coffee," Dottie said, mingling and speaking loudly to the guests. "Or hell, wine and beer."

There was a little cheer from most, a groan from Raymond.

"But. I have to charge you for any hard liquor. I'm not the owner, you understand. It's not my stuff to give. If you steal, I'll have to pay and if I can't, I'll be sent to jail."

"Hey, but what *isn't* jail, really?" asked someone from the rock band.

"You may be right about that. Still. The Cape Head jail has no TV. And the beds are hard as boards, I hear. Nor do they give you a pillow," said Dottie.

The aqua lobby—with the strange people and the peach-colored light from the fire and wall lamps, and with Dottie seeming readied for a date—became a distorted version of the lobby, to me like a colorized film.

Now Dottie was announcing to the room: "Last spring before the red-tide law there was a huge storm and afterwards a smorgasbord washed up—short lobsters, which're illegal. Jackknife clams and ocean clams, not so good. But

Subtraction

cherrystone and blue clams. I filled up twelve trash bags and I have a freezer full of chowder. I should go warm the restaurant's stove burners."

Raymond swept her under his arm and toward me for a whispered conference.

"Clam chowder? Mom, what're you thinking?" I asked.

"Keep them busy so they don't steal us blind and rape us."

Raymond said, "This way, they'll rape you on full stomachs, with more energy."

We looked over at the storm victims.

The teenage girl, lifting her mime-mask face, held up her stick and rocked it back and forth like the needle of a metronome.

"Bus crash on the way to the bughouse," I sang. "All the inmates here at the inn . . ."

"I can handle them," Dottie said.

"As you've been doing! Why not throw them a clambake."

"Oh, lay off that, Paige. I was only going to feed them. The chowder might be contaminated anyway," she said.

"Atta way, Mom, give them salmonella."

"What you two should do is smoke some of my Colombian," Dottie said. "There's a shoebox of it left, and believe me, it helps."

The walls outside the Colonel's Suite wore faded paper with an egg-and-dart pattern. On the north wall an aneroid barometer said the air pressure was falling fast. It was dusk.

I swung open the suite's door.

Balanced on the vanity was Raymond. He held a Bible, didn't turn his head, but said, "Hi ya, Paige."

The sea window on the far wall vibrated. Its shutters

were latched, nailed, and ribbons of caulking were plugged all around the inside glass, yet the window rocked tensely in the wall.

"You ever read the conversion tables, back of the Gideon? Like the weights and measures? Says one talent's the equal of seventy-five pounds. Or a shekel's same as two-fifths an ounce. Now, a handbreadth . . ."

I slid down the wall like a thrown plateful of noodles, and said from the floor, "I'm flattered and grateful that you came a million miles in a holocaust just to visit me, Raymond."

"But?"

"Why did you? I don't mean that how it sounds. But why did you?"

"I felt dirt miserable about scarin' you off," he said and shrugged. "And wanted to see you."

I said, "I'm glad you came. Which is wrong. I shouldn't be . . ."

We could hear the voices of more people arriving; hear Dottie chattering.

"Get up on the bed," Raymond said, as he hopped from the vanity. He dead-bolted the door.

Raymond awakened as I slid from under the quilt out into the ferocious cold of the drafty room.

"Time is it?" he asked with his eyes closed.

"Only four-thirty or five, but it's getting dark. Sorry I woke you."

" 'S all right. Snap in and out. Haven't really *slept* since my drinking slip. That's the problem with me."

"Only problem," I said, pulling on my T-shirt. I looped the silver chain with Raf's miraculous medal around my neck. I always wore the medal but it hid under my clothes.

"Lemme see that," Raymond said.

The storm was hammering the inn. Above the wind's roar, there were thuds as strayed tree limbs slammed the walls. From a floor above came a little shattering noise, the explosion of window glass.

Raymond examined the medal.

I said, "Raf gave that to me. He claims it's what's kept him alive through wars and vile presidents."

" 'O Mary conceived without sin . . .' " Raymond read aloud. "Some break, no original sin. Hell of a starting discount," he said.

"I don't know," I said, taking back the medal. "It doesn't seem right using this as a lucky piece."

I went to the window, cranked it open, unlatched and pounded apart the shutters. I whirl-whipped the chain a few revolutions and cast the medal into the snow in the side yard.

"Don't worry, it wasn't blessed by priests or anything," I told Raymond. "Although Raf probably dunked it in drinks and baptized it a few times."

Raymond emerged smiling from the shower, wearing my blue terrycloth bathrobe and his head in a towel burnoose.

"What kind of band *are* they?" I asked, from a cross-legged position on the bed.

"Gimme me the choices," Raymond said.

"Well, I don't know what's up with bands these days. I suppose they could be political, or heavy metal thrash, or postmodern punk, or retro-paisley-acid rock, or a neo-folk group, like troubadours."

Raymond shook off the towel and used it to blot his hair. He said, "The first thing is, they don't have guitars or drums or nothin'. And they can't sing; they couldn't carry a tune in a Peterbilt truck. They're bankrolled by one of 'em's father—that one that wears the beret? What *he* told me is they're a theoretical band out on a theoretical tour. Which all just means they don't play music, but talk about how they *would* play it if they was real, not theoretical."

"Yeah, but, Raymond, think of all the bad songs they're sparing the world," I said.

"It's a quieter, better place," he said.

I said, "In fact, I wish there were theoretical poets who never wrote. That'd clear the decks for me. What's the name of the band?"

"None. The beret guy said a name would legitimize 'em as havin' a profit motive, and that'd make them whores of commerce. But I believe they tried thinking of a name, and couldn't come up with any," Raymond said.

The band and other storm victims were in the sitting room now, dozing or drowsily watching flames snap on the driftwood in the fireplace.

I went past them and into a utility closet. I gathered flashlights, boxes of storm candles, every filled hurricane lamp. In three trips I toted the stuff to the registry desk. I buckled on a belt with an encased flashlight, and pocketed a box of blue-tip stick matches.

Dottie already had a flashlight and lamps waiting on her nightstand in the Commodore's Suite. She was watching her portable TV: the Patriots losing to the Jets.

Fredo rested on his side, half under the bed's pinwheel quilt.

Without much notice, Dottie was smoking a joint and,

with her free hand, stroking Fredo's ear. "So, Paige," she said to me. "You've got problems."

"Two problems, yes," I said.

"Stop him! Stop him!" Dottie yelled at the television. She drew on her cigarette. "Don't ask what *I'd* do, I'm in the same position. Between Mario and Paul? You couldn't know Paul. He's a fellow I date, a vet from Hampham. I mean a *pet* vet. Anyway, the point is . . . just a second. First and ten, way to go! What *they* do decides . . . I've forgotten what."

I said, "So have I. Blow that stuff the other way, Mother. Couldn't I just live here and have Raymond and Raf take turns visiting me?"

"It would have to count as both your birthday and Christmas presents," Dottie said.

"Raf's a bad husband," I said. "I deserve a good husband. Why do I still want Raf?"

"He's an awfully good time," Dottie said.

Fredo stirred and peered about as if looking for something.

"Your jingle ball's in the kitchen," my mother told him.

The dog disappeared, whimpering as he hunted his toy.

"Let me ask something," I said. "Did it ever bother you, Mario's being known as an artist and that his statues and sculptures will endure long beyond us?"

"Bother me? No. Oh, no. I couldn't live with it, though; I had to make my own way."

The lights went, and as the blowers on the furnace died I heard a sagging noise. I was traveling a dim hall. I set down my lamp, removed its glass chimney, adjusted the frayed wick, fired it with a stick match.

In the lamp's light, moving toward the kitchen, I fitted storm candles into the inkwell-like holders along the way.

"I knew it," Dottie said in the kitchen. "Fourth down, seventy-five yards from their own end zone, fourth quarter, power out."

Her face in the lamp shadow seemed one-dimensional.

She twisted a stove knob and a burner's blue ring of flame rose with a poof. "Gas is O.K. I'll go see about the pilot."

Her mules bonked on the stairs down to the dirt-floored cellar. She called back, "The furnace has an electric pilot but you can relight the ignition by hand!"

The rectangular window over the sink was vaguely green and smeared with the reflection of my lamp.

I heard Dottie swear. I heard a whimpered curse. From far down on the Point Road I heard sirens, but their shrieks got no closer and intermixed with the yowling wind.

Raymond appeared. In the light wash, his suntan deepened, his teeth looked more even and white. "What's happening? I heard a snowplow."

I said, "I think it's the Mass. troopers, trying to clear the Point Road. Then the salt and sand crews'll try to keep it clear."

I ladled chowder into mugs. My hair got moist from the soup's steam. My sweatshirt had the smell of burnt hickory.

Behind me stood Pat Gilly, a lobsterman from the village. In his fist he squeezed a bulky stein that brimmed with frothy beer. Pat had ginger hair, freckles, a lot of size.

For the third time he said, "By God, I love your big ass, Paige."

"Thank you again, Pat."

"This is the worst since seventy-eight. In that one, we lost every tree in our yard and half the roof of our house. What a girl you are, tall as I am, only smart."

"Thanks, Pat. Drink up."

I loaded two more cups of chowder and passed them to Heather, the brawny teenager from the rock band. She'd been helping me.

"I like bein' your assistant, but I miss my shaking stick," Heather said. "It burned up."

"We'll get you another. Just take those around and hand them to somebody," I said.

"I'm beach trash," said Pat Gilly.

"Me too," I said.

Pat said, "But I'm God-fearing. I fear God and I pray. I'm not ashamed of it."

"Me neither. You should go check on your kids, Pat. See that they have blankets and pillows and something to eat."

"They ate. They ate before the wagon brought us over," Pat said.

"Then you could make sure each has had his goodnight kick in the head," I said.

"Look at your ass," Pat said. "You are the girlie!"

"Pat, here comes your wife. I think it's your wife and she's gonna hear you praising my buttocks."

"She ain't here, she dropped over in the saloon. Anyway, she knows I like your big butt."

"I'm careless with hot stuff. Really sloppy with it. You should stay back," I said.

Dottie surfaced in the kitchen, dusting her palms, her face flushed and merry. "Everybody's fed, just about. We have three more arriving from the Will O'Lee Rest Home. The Petkin boys are out on ski-mobiles collecting folks.

I'm giving away gallons of beer. Want me to help bowl that chowder?"

"No, but you could kill Pat for me. All he'll talk about is my can."

"In jest, Dot," Pat Gilly said.

"Act right," she told him.

"With Paige? Hell, I'm friends with her husband. Raf and me are great friends!"

"Shut up about him," I said, and left the kitchen.

In the taproom, there were twenty or so blanket cocoons on the floor. People stood or leaned. Couples held on to one another. Two Gilly children squirted by.

I saw a few older women from the village. "So kind of your mother," one said as I passed.

A second asked, "Sweetheart? Do you have any aspirin?"

"In a minute. Can you wait a little bit?"

"Cold twists my bones," the woman said.

I stepped over a body wrapped in an afghan.

Drafts leaking from the loose front entrance doors kept the foyer cleared, but a crowd had formed in the sitting room, where the fireplace flared and candles were glowing. The restaurant beyond was crammed. In there, women stood on line for the washroom.

I made it to the Admiral's Suite and showered. I ate a tangerine in the hot spray, pinched the rind and dripped juice onto my head as a hair rinse.

Shadows blackened the bedroom. I groped around, clenching a towel at my chest.

Just before dawn I woke with my head on Raymond's bare shoulder, his arm caught under me.

In the dark, I found my flashlight belt and dressed; tiptoed out and walked the egg-and-dart-papered hall.

There were sleeping bodies everywhere now: in the tap-room, on the bar itself, behind the bar. In the sitting room, swaddled bodies lay on the couches and crisscrossed on the rugs. The fire was down to a last bump of smoldering wood.

I kept my flashlight's beam lowered but here and there shined on a startled face.

In a corner, a young couple chatted. Near them, a woman rocked an infant in her arms.

All the storm candles had burned away.

Dottie leaned on the mantel. I went near, and when she said nothing, I tipped my flashlight up at her profile. She was asleep.

"You're some kind of horse," I said.

"I'm right here," she muttered.

"No you're not, Mom. Go to bed."

"I'm standing watch."

"You'll be no good to anybody tomorrow. It *is* tomorrow. You must hurt and you must be wrecking your poor legs."

She had me follow her into the chilly hallway, away from the crowd. "The furnace is giving us a little heat but the blowers are out. It's going to stay bitter cold all morning. We're down to instant coffee but we have tea. It's stale, but nobody'll know the difference." She heaved a deep breath and hugged herself, hugged the sleeves of her navy-blue cardigan. "What else? We're out of fruit juice and yogurt," she said.

At sunup, the winds calmed, the snow stopped. The storm had passed.

I waded all over the side yard, searching with my flashlight. It felt eighty below and my cheeks froze and stuck to my stocking mask after ten minutes of burrowing, but I recovered Raf's miraculous medal and hung the icy stiff chain on my neck.

Monday morning had the festive oddness of a canceled business day.

The storm victims had drunk the entire beer supply and two kegs of hard cider that Dottie stored last Halloween.

Many of those milling in the main house were hung over and ill, or just impatient to get home and start digging out.

I went for a short hike to see if the roads were clear enough for Raf to manage.

The bluffs were frosted with ice and snow. The sky had crude ashy strokes that were backlit and ember-orange. Pinned to the horizon was a cargo ship that had ridden out last night's weather.

I saw below, rumbling around on the Point Road, troopers, gargantuan sand trucks, a couple of uniformed National Guard.

Raymond helped me cook breakfast. We made gallons of tea, heated biscuits and chick peas with chicken gravy.

"Something I've never seen," Raymond said. "Eight industrial-sized cans of chick peas."

CARE

THE LIGHTS came back on and the TV over the bar started talking. There were cheers and shouts from all over the first floor.

"That was fast, actually," Dottie said.

"Tell *me*," said a villager. "In seventy-eight we were down for nine goddamn days."

I went to the Admiral's Suite, to my room, and found four kids up on the bed playing a card game.

"See if you can find your parents," I said. "Because I think you get to go home now."

I picked up the phone, heard a dial tone, tried my Brookline number.

I got a ring.

"Yeah?" said a groggy Raf.

"Are you with anyone?"

"Just the triplets. What're *you* doing?"

"I've been looking for you for months," I said.

"You're at the Seahorse? I tried to get out there. We had a touch of bad weather."

"Making *me* call *you*," I said. "I'm hanging up."

"Wait, wait, wait, wait."

"No. Sorry to bother you, go back to sleep," I said.

"The fucking phone was out, in fact. And I have no ground transportation," Raf said. "Last night, swear to God, I tried to *walk* to the inn."

"Well, if that's true, it was dumb."

"It was love," he said.

On my dresser stood the wine bottle Raymond had de-labeled and not drunk.

I said, "Don't start doing this. It's really not fair."

"I made it to Storrow Drive, then the ninety-three entrance but nothing was moving. And I was getting disoriented, like hypothermia. My brain went white although I was *sober*, speaking of *not fair*. Then this Triple-A truck with chains picks me up and brings me back as far as Boylston and I hiked on home. Look at my fucking fingers!"

"What?" I said. "Black?"

"No, but quivering. They'll feel a lot better once they get into your jeans."

Raymond moseyed into the room and stood behind me in the mirror. "*There* you are," he said.

"Look, Raf," I said into the phone, and Raymond slumped. "I just don't know anymore, you know?"

Raf said, "I do. I know for both of us, is the great thing."

Raymond hunted around the vanity table, picked up a vagrant cigarette and slanted it behind his ear.

"Paige? This goddamned storm, I mean, it was ill timed," said Raf.

I sighed. I said, "I'll try to make it into Cambridge. You could meet me at the faculty club."

"Aw, not the fuckin' fac . . ." Raf groaned before I put out his voice with mine.

"Raymond's here," I said.

Raymond made signals at me. "No, no, I don't want to talk to him," the signals said.

There was nothing from Raf's end for a bit. "Pru with him?" he said, finally.

"No. Evidently that's over."

"So he's with you," Raf said.

"Since the storm, yeah. He came up and he's been with me," I said.

Now Raf sighed. He said, "Well, you needn't think of it as a storm, Paige. More as a kind of winter carnival. Every goddamn dream-come-true. We need to fuckin' talk! So how is the old singing cowboy? Diggin' in those spurs?"

"Don't you dare," I said. "Where have *you* been?"

"I'd have to hire a detective to tell *me* for the first part of where I've been, but I think some Mexico was involved, and I either got elected to office in this little town or I was detained in their jail."

"If I were betting, I know where I'd put my money."

"All I remember is a courthouse. And then I was exported, probably. And anyway, ever after, I've been hanging with Mario."

"Mario!"

"Yeah. He who bounced you on his knee?"

"A lie," I said.

"No, it's true, you can ask him. I like his place. We could live in Providence. You ever thought about moving there?"

I said, "The faculty club about five and leave your suggestions with the triplets."

Raymond broke in. "What suggestions?" he asked me. "Is he giving you trouble?"

"I heard that," Raf said on the phone.

By noontime, most of the emergency guests were gone. The rock band had left, Raymond told me; left in a group, and not in theory but in fact.

"Aw, and I never got to know them," I said.

Walt Barber, the Cape Head policeman, showed up along with a young highway patrolman. Walt looked pasty, red-eyed. He hadn't shaved in a while. "I'll take tea, coffee, Coke, anything with zip," he said.

The patrolman said, "We're lucky. Everything's melting. The armory's about emptied out. We can run whoever left down there. We got supplies for them. Roads to Was-nascawa are clear."

"Good work, boys," Dottie said.

"Nobody's slept," Walt Barber said. "I wish I could've been here last night. Appears you had like a New Year's Eve party."

"Not too bad," Dottie said.

"You won't get paid back for it, though."

"I know," she said.

Walt Barber said, "You can try. But you know the condition of the Cape Head coffers." He stood erect and turned out his empty trouser pockets.

"I know that," Dottie said.

He nodded, bit down a yawn. "Phew, I'm an old fucking guy."

"Watch that mouth," Dottie told him.

The patrolman said, "I've heard such words before, ma'am, believe me."

I asked, "If I tried to get into the city, could I make it?"

"I'd say fifty-fifty. I'd say don't try, unless it's an emergency," Walt Barber sad.

I looked over at Raymond, leaning on a wall in all his Southwestern colors, haggard and handsome.

"It's an emergency," I said.

I squished out to the Dutch barn, got positioned in the smoke-colored car, fired up the engine, and waited for the heater to breathe warm before chugging around front to collect Raymond.

"Life's *harder* up here," he said. "I'm facing Raf, and this faculty-club place where they'll make me eat in the basement. I'm freezing all the time. For doin' the littlest thing I gotta wear all my clothes and never mind what I *wanna* wear, you know? Now we'll most probably slide over a cliff."

His voice came out stuttered from his shaking. His teeth knocked.

I drove the Point Road. The wind combing the bluffs still blew snow. There were steel-colored puddles with ice skins.

A chain wrestled and clanged on the flagpole outside the Wasnascawa post office.

In Hampham, kids' crayon drawings of winter were taped to the windows of the grade school. The pictures had snowmen with carrot noses; scribbled figures swerving on skates; hooded men teetering on skis.

People were shoveling furiously. Repair trucks worked over every wire and pole. Fallen tree branches lay on side roads. A lone salt and sand truck had most of the driving space on the main drag and ahead of him was a monster plow. It trapped rows of cars at street meters, putting them behind a snow mountain and covering some entirely.

I drove off the peninsula, past the ROUTE 20A sign, which bled rust from its borders.

In the rearview now I could see the shanking leg-shaped peninsula—bay side and ocean—and there were boats and towers, tiny rooftops, soft brown clouds of trees.

"How's it driving?" asked Raymond.

"O.K. so far," I said, although the road was cracked, crumbling at the shoulders, pocked with deep holes where it surfaced at all.

"You still like me?" he asked.

Because of the road I could spare only a glance, but he had invested a lot in the question, I could see.

I nodded. "A lot." I said.

Away from the beach there was no mist and the street shone with sunlight.

In Boston, on the BU bridge, cars were confined to one lane and being flagged slowly, singly. Emergency crews worked behind crusty metal cones. There were winking Day-Glo lights, caution signs. Still, the city was open for business.

The desk officer shook dry the check I had inked to get my club privileges unsuspended. "I don't know if I have the authority to *decide* this," she was saying.

She wore three sweaters—thick and thin cardigans and a pullover—and tiny glasses on a necklace chain.

Raf had long been using my ID number and signing for drinks and food in the downstairs bar and cafeteria.

"I don't know if I've ever *seen* a bar bill this large," the desk officer said.

We waited in the velvet-draperied reading room, a half-dozen dons and Raymond and I, drinking coffee from a silver pot and china cups. The profs turned newspapers, folded them, dozed.

"I'm just here to fix the furnace," Raymond whispered to me.

"Relax."

"No, I'm just the pest exterminator, if anyone asks you. I came about roach control."

He followed me over to a bow window. We watched bundled-up literature students rushing in and out of Warren House; watched young women treading snow. They wore cheap white yarn gloves, metal-tipped cowboy boots, down jackets opened at the throat on their grandmothers' pearls.

A chime called us to dinner.

We let ourselves be guided across the maroon carpeting to a corner table. The room had scarlet linen and miniature paintings beaming with lacquer, long windows, and a view of a forty-foot hemlock in the yard.

"O.K., so you'll help me with which fork and all, right?" Raymond said.

"This place, I think they *give* you only one fork," I said.

We ate iced oysters with hot sauce.

"Raf!" Raymond said.

I shucked another oyster. "He better show up," I said.

Raf lifted me up out of my chair and turned me around. He folded his arms over my shoulders and kissed me. He smelled clean, of the outdoors and winter. On his hands were big gloves of wet leather, which he kept, fingers spread, away from his embrace.

I pulled back, and saw that he looked gaunt but darkly appealing. A long chesterfield topcoat hung from his shoulders.

"I remember you," I said.

He shrugged and gave me his crinkly grin.

"Lifeboy!" he shouted at Raymond. The other diners twisted in their seats.

"Raf, Jesus," I muttered.

He lunged at Raymond in a half-fall, and hugged him. "Didn't we cut a swath down on the bayous?" Raf said.

"Turn me loose," said Raymond. "Let go."

Raf did. He swirled out my chair and I got resettled.

His own seat he jammed between Raymond and me. He crossed his legs knee on knee, flapped open his napkin, and dropped it over his lap. He removed neither his coat, muffler, nor gloves.

"June, how are your boys?" he asked our waitress.

"Oh no, you," she said to Raf. She was a woman about Dottie's age, in a simple woolen dress with a corsage.

" 'S all right, I'm sober. Bring us seared beef tips and glazed carrots. You'll love those, Ray. And that lawn-mower-bottom spinach."

"My youngest got accepted at Notre Dame," June told Raf.

"Eureka!" he shouted.

While we waited for our food, Raf talked to us or to himself aloud. He talked about signs and signifiers, reflexive texts, Italian cinema, public sculpture, and private interests.

"Sir, don't touch the plate. It's very hot," June said, as

she delivered Raymond's platter of crackling meat and vegetables. She positioned the plate with an oven mitten.

Raymond moved the platter, getting it lined up in front of him. "Yow!" he yelled.

"She warned you," said Raf.

"Yeah, Raymond, that's why Raf kept his gloves on for the meal," I said.

Raymond dunked his hand in his ice-water glass. He said, "You're bein' real cute, Raf, but there's something we all should be saying."

Raf got busy cutting his food—all of it—down to morsels. He didn't eat, but carpentered his food with fork and knife, sawing and dividing.

As he worked, I said, "Well, Raymond's right, of course."

"You're this way now, Raf, but you keep buggin' out on her."

"Raymond, I better do this," I said.

Raf was slicing his baby carrots into paper-thin slivers.

"It's agony being your wife," I said.

A waiter interrupted to ask if we needed more coffee. Raf tinked his coffee saucer with his knife, nodded yes.

"Acting on impulse," I said, "and with no sense of responsibility . . . it's fun for a while. But it's not too practical, or considerate, and it gets to be . . ."

"When the years start adding up and the wisdom doesn't," Raymond said.

"Well, there I disagree," I said. "The years have nothing to do with it."

"I didn't mean you're old, Paige. I meant our health is going."

"I'm in great health!" I said.

"I didn't mean your health. I meant Raf's."

I said, "But that's Raf's concern. That's not what I'm arguing. Not like, grow up and get healthy."

"No, never that!" Raymond said. "Like to see the day either one of you grows up and acts your goddamn age."

"Look, Raf can act any way he wants, do whatever he wants. But he can't expect me to hang around in the margins of his life ready with aspirin and checkbook," I said.

"He's gonna die of it," Raymond said. "If you cared about him like I do, you'd want him to knock it off."

"That's his decision to make," I said.

"You expect *him* to make a decision. Look at him!"

We looked at Raf. He had a plate of confetti food and a knife in his left glove, a fork in his right. He blinked back at us, as if he hadn't been paying much attention.

"Raf," I said. "When you next go wildcatting or on some chase, hold it in mind that I won't be around when it's over. I'll be off doing what I need to do."

"But you already did," Raf said. "You fucked Raymond."

"None of your business," I said, and Raymond growled in exasperation.

"I think I'll get June and send this meat back," Raf said. "It's too tiny."

"Why don't I want to kill him and blind his other eye?" Raymond asked me. "The whole long drive in, all I dreamed about was killing him, blinding him, and tearing off his goddamned ears."

"It's because deep down we're still flower children," Raf said.

"Why don't you tear off just one ear," I said to Raymond.

Raf said, "Let's get out of here and go *eat*. Raymond, you've never seen our Brookline place, have you?"

———

We walked among a pack of grad students who were wearing buckled rubber boots and flight jackets: folks who'd come from the film labs at Sever or down from the architecture library in Gund.

"There's a reading at the Grolier," one of them said to me. It was Herb, the computer-whiz who'd booked my Houston flight. He went along with us as far as Mass. Ave.

"A poetry reading? Are you going, Herb?" I asked.

"Hell no, you kidding?" he said.

"We haven't met," Raf said. "I'm Paige's husband Raf, and this is her husband Raymond, and you're her husband . . . Herb, is it?"

Raf curbed the car illegally in front of our Brookline place, a three-story house on a street of tall houses that crowded each other and were crowded by towering trees. Ours was painted lemon with ivy-colored trim. There were sun porches and overhangs, today dripping ice.

"I didn't expect it to look like this," Raymond said. "Homey."

Inside, he prowled the rooms. He paused at a wall of built-in bookshelves. "You read all these poetry books?"

"They're written by friends, mostly," I said.

"Ha! If they were really your friends, they wouldn't commit poetry," Raf said.

We climbed to the top floor, where the rooms had views of downtown Boston.

Raymond and Raf strolled into my study—a long white-walled rectangle where I kept my typewriter, reference

books, filing cabinets, class schedules, ledgers, appointment calendars.

"It's *nice*," Raymond said.

"It is nice and she keeps it tidy. But notice everything's all dusty?" Raf said. "Neat and nice but dusty."

Raymond tapped his index finger on an oil-chalk drawing, framed and mounted on one white plaster wall. "You did this, right?" he asked Raf.

"*She* did it," Raf said.

"Shut up," I said.

"Is it art?" asked Raymond.

"History will have to answer that question," said Raf. "I think it's her drawing of, I think, a kid pulling a wagon. I think."

Raymond leaned back and squinted with his left eye, now with his right. "I sort of see the wagon part," he said.

We ordered Indian food and sat in the living room waiting for the delivery. The day darkened, but no one turned on a light.

"Don't you all have a television?"

Raf said there was a black-and-white in a closet upstairs. He said it was a deleterious appliance, in his opinion. "*This* television," he said, "won't do anything but show television shows."

Raymond looked around. His fingers clawed the cloth on his knee. "I never pictured this," he said. "I thought you two would travel lighter, is all. You got an *existence* here."

I slept on the couch, wearing a sturdy bra, a T-shirt, underpants, tights, socks, a sweat suit, and a bundling of

quilts and blankets, although the steam radiator was pounding out heat. I knotted the pillow case in my fist and squeezed shut my eyes.

Raymond closed himself in the spare bedroom for the night, and Raf, the last I noticed, was stalking around under the headphones of a cassette player, smoking a cigarette, drinking from a stein of coffee.

"Animals not human, they stand like this, see?" Mario said. He got down on all fours. He let his head hang. "A dog, a horse, a mule. Lookata where my face sees. Sees *down*, right?"

"Dad, get up," I said.

"But a human," Mario said, "gotta sightline right on da horizon."

Mario pulled up to a standing posture.

"When you work with mass and big big weight, see, and balance, you wonder, my God, how come you have something weighs two hundred pounds and can stand and move around on two small pads!" He walked around his kitchen, demonstrating the miracle of locomotion.

"Move around, walk around, get the salt, move around," he continued. "And not fall over?"

"You couldn't weigh two hundred pounds," Raymond said.

"No, I talk about Paige," Mario said. He grabbed me from behind, hooped me at the waist and bear-hugged me.

"Look at this animal," Mario said. "She's no good, but sheeza fun to squeeze."

Raf exchanged a dry look with Raymond.

Mario picked up my hands, as if I were a dummy. He raised a hand and spoke for me but in his own voice. "I'm

named Paige," Mario said, waving my hand, hello, at Raf and Raymond. "Sometimes, my pretty mother moves me around and other times my genius father. But when they go off busy I live in a closet and think up my own stupid songs."

"Huh," Raf said, interested.

"Sometimes," Mario said, "is a crazy guy, sick awhen he was just a boy, got only one eye drags me outa the closet. We walk around, move around, get the salt, get the pepper, move a left foot, move a right, eat some good food." Mario made my hand jerk up and address my face, as if I were shoveling in mouthfuls of food.

"This explains a lot," Raymond said.

"Then, all done, I go to sleep," Mario said. He reached around and gently shut my eyelids with the tips of his callused fingers. "And I'm asleep and sleep and dream of when I was a fish, who is how I start out my life as. A fish, same as everybody."

"You're damn straight," Raf said.

We moved into Mario's living room, which was huge and not empty, but seemed empty. The blond-wood floors had a high gloss and were unmarked. There was a stepladder my father had painted red. On a long shelf sat the pieces of his complicated stereo system. In a corner, in a ceramic tub, posed a lemon tree. Lined up side by side against a blank wall were five old white leather armchairs.

The three of us took seats in three of these. Mario perched on the stepladder. "You gotta lot of power here," he said to me. "In this room, Paige, you got power."

"That's news to me," I said.

"No," he said. "It isn't. Who wants music? Who wants I make some stew?"

"Who wants you talk like an American?" I snapped.

My father said, "Some kittens, you think, why didn't I drowned it when I had da chance? Hey, Raymond, you gotta little daughter, yes?"

"You gotta meet her mom and dad before you get a fix on Paige," Raf said.

"I got my own fix already," said Raymond.

We were out in Mario's yard, looking west over a downhill forest of pines to a country road. East were the four ribbons of Route 95.

"You ever read her poetry?" Raf asked.

"Sure. It was good. Wasn't very forthcoming. Nothin' in it about herself, but I liked it," Raymond said. He turned to me. "Do *you* like it?"

"My own poetry? I couldn't say. It's just mine, like the family dog."

Mario fed us a stew flavored deeply with wine, onions, dark tastes.

Afterward, he hummed while serving bowls of his spicy, black, blistering-hot coffee.

"You saw Mom last month," I said.

"No."

"She told me about it. In Boston. You two went out."

"I couldn't see her," Mario said, and he looked sad. "She was so dressed up."

On the drive from Mario's, Raf told about a spot in Mexico where the surfing was good but the beach was crowded by pigs eating litter. He said he came back over the border at El Paso, and went on north across the Great Plains with a seventy-year-old woman who rinsed her mouth with Scotch and drove a used, repainted, resold police car.

"There's a ride I'm just as glad I missed," Raymond said.

Raf said he got a New York train in Chicago, a Boston train in New York, but had to get off, sick, in Providence.

"So naturally I called Mario. And he tells me, 'Raffo! But sure. We fix you like a hole.'"

"Whole, as in complete and entire?" I asked.

"No, he meant like a hole in the ground," Raf said.

"That's how I always think of you," Raymond said.

Raf said, "Turns out, he meant literally—as literal as he gets. This was October when the ground was still workable and he had me dig a pond for him. More like a lake. With a shovel and wheelbarrow and pickaxe. And then he had me fill it back up. I got plenty sober, I promise," Raf said.

"But, Raf, you forgot to stay down *in the hole* when you covered it," said Raymond.

MATTER

DOTTIE greeted us at the service delivery door around midnight. She wore a little makeup, her satin robe and slippers. I had phoned from Mario's to say we were coming.

"Raf! Wow!" she said, embracing him. "You had us so scared."

"I'm fine," he said, "You been smoking stuff, Dottie?"

"Naw," she said, and hugged Raymond.

"Hey, Pretty," Raymond said.

"Don't chew your hair," Dottie told me.

Raymond said, "We figured we could help you straighten up some after the storm crowd."

"You can, you can. Great. *God* yes."

We had agreed to sit here in Dottie's suite, away from the saloon and the taproom.

"And it's too long since you and I shot the bull," said Raf.

"You are the one with words," Dottie said. "You always were."

I said, "Thank you, Mother. Considering I'm a poet."

"You all been to visit my ex?"

"Yeah, wonderful guy," Raymond said. "But I can see how you'd get worn out with him."

Dottie tilted her head left and right, the way Fredo did when some sound had him puzzled.

"I didn't mean nothin' bad," Raymond said. His drawl seemed thicker, or maybe like his sun colors, just more noticeable out of his home context.

"Mario did not wear me out," Dottie said.

Raymond blinked sadly. He said, "I have not been able to say one thing I meant since I crossed over the Mason-Dixon. I believe the cold weather's freeze-dried my brain —'specially the part that's in charge of word choice."

"I've read about that. Happens often to Southerners," Raf said. "They get more Southern."

"It's a defense," Raymond said.

"The defense may rest," Raf told him.

"Raf's actually named Walter," I said. "That's his real name, in case either of you didn't know."

"Walter?" Raymond said.

"I *didn't* know," said Dottie. "That's awful. But never mind, you're still Raf to us."

"Walter?" Raymond said again.

"And just when I was on your side," Raf said to me.

In the morning, the rooms were sunny, the sky outside a cloudless blue. The four of us set to work.

We laundered blankets and bed linens, drop cloths for the furniture.

Raf drove me and Fredo into Hampham to replenish Dottie's personal refrigerator and the hotel stock that the storm victims used. We bought candles, lamp oil, batteries;

pounds of coffee, rice, beans, and flour. We bought ba-
guettes and éclairs at the bakery, and fish fillets and sweet
peppers at South Shore Market.

On the ride back to Cape Head, I said, "Raf, we don't
have to get a divorce."

"All right. I wasn't thinking we did, but all right."

"I'll be around," I said. "And you can visit, and stay
or not. We just won't be an act; we're breaking up the
act."

"All right," he said, and blew air out his cheeks.

"Nothing's expected of you, so there's nothing to run
from. No reason to lie or hide what you do anymore."

"I know."

"Of course, this is both of us. You can't expect anything
from *me*."

"I'm sorry to cut in here," Raf said. "But way out there
on the bay, that spouting thing? You think that could be
a whale?"

Dottie wok-fried the fish we bought, and now the four of
us gathered for supper. The group's personality was different, though. We concentrated on eating, tearing through
the meal.

To fill air, I talked about quarks, and Barny, the physicist. I said that must have been something, finding a whole
new layer, the deepest level of matter. "A thing less than
a millionth of an atom in size," I said.

Raymond didn't speak at all. I saw in his eyes what I
sometimes saw in Raf's, that he was already off and traveling. I'd catch him studying me, and I could see that he
didn't want to go, in some ways, but that in all ways, he
needed to.

———

Dottie and I shared a joint. We were in the sitting room off the lobby, with candlelight twinkling on the cherry wood and on the tall ships' portraits and on the plasticky flanks of the big fish mounted over the mantel.

For a frozen few moments, I thought my mom looked as though she were mourning something and that her head was lowered in sorrow. I heard crying. The moments, suspended for me and set off in brackets from time flow, ended when the crying shaped itself around a gull somewhere in the distance.

In my sleep, I had pictures of back roads crunchy with salt, sawtooth warehouse roofs; and last of Connie, Raymond's dog, falling seven stories, exploding in starbursts and dust where her shadow had been, leaving a steel trash can in a papery crumple.

Raymond booked an eleven-o'clock flight out of Logan, and Raf did a gallant thing, insisting he had leg cramps from his dawn run on the beach.

"You two go alone," he said. "I don't want to anyway. It's a goddamned gruesome drive."

He said goodbye to Raymond in the foyer of the inn. "Hoss," he said.

"Hoss," said Raymond.

"If you happen into Pru down there . . ."

Raymond said, "Pru and me, we'll be all right after a while, after I get over the urge to drop her off some tower. I could marry her now, would be one way to go. Luisa and I are done with business. Her intended's the lawyer did our divorce. Pru would rebel but deep inside it's what she wants—marriage, quit her job, a dad for Lilith, some taste of calm."

"We all acted pretty stupid," Raf said. "Next time, we'll just talk about how stupid we were."

"No," Raymond said.

Every mile I drove toward Logan, I felt a sad panic. "There must be something of dying in this," I told Raymond. "Maybe why people make those we'll-call-every-day promises."

"Right," he said.

"You want to make sure the other keeps on . . ."

"Right."

"It's funny, my staying with Dottie and Raf's gonna be at Mario's. Like we went home to Mom and Dad," I said.

"That's funny," Raymond said.

"Until we grow up, as you suggested."

Raymond put on his dictator dark glasses and lit a cigarette. He smoothed back his sunny hair. He said, "I remember I walked into that cantina and seen you last summer shaking in your booth, and I told myself, 'Raymond, you move real slow on this one 'cause she'll spook like a rabbit. She'll go streaming off like a rabbit.' "

"You were such a gent," I said.

"You know, except when you were on the road, we been together almost every day since?"

I hadn't realized that, but it explained why, on safari in my backthoughts, was the idea that Raymond would stay with me. I said, "I'll pay. I'm serious, I'll pay for the flight if you'll come back next weekend or the one after."

"I need to get with my crew and work. And I ran through most of my savings. Gotta replace my car," Raymond said.

"But what's important, finally?" I asked.

"Important? Walking upright. Havin' a daughter. I got all your dad's signals. Not so stupid as Raf thinks."

"I can't stand this," I said.

"I lied about your poetry," Raymond said. "I don't like it. You aren't in it, or maybe you'd say there's some coded version, but fuck that. My tastes, whatever thing you make *is* you, no mistaking it."

I winced but set a little smile.

"You should've been different with me, Paige. You got a nice inn to go to, and a sit-down horseshit job, and Raf's got your dad backin' him up, but what I do sort of counts."

"Like leaving Luisa and moving in with Pru?" I said.

Raymond huffed and cranked his window and fired away his cigarette.

"That's for me to live with and for you it's that you could've been different. I hope it eats at you. I hope you wake up crying for me. Because you won't ever see me again. And you can't rectify anything and Raf can't be my friend 'cause you can't edit or change what's over."

He wouldn't let me walk in with him at Logan, or even park the car. He yanked his bag—a canvas carpenter's tote—from the back seat and swung into daylight. He said nothing. I watched him join the hectic current of traffic at the passenger drop-off. I saw that his clothes were too frail for even this milder northern day, that the back of his unlined jacket still had a powdering of construction dust. His Levi's puckered where his knee poked through, and there was red Texas mud frozen to his boot heel. The wind roughed his hair and it flared for a second before he was gone through the terminal doors.

———

The last step in my setting up a work space at the inn was plugging in Raymond's gift computer. Its small screen flushed amber as the machine powered up.

"If you're going to stay long, you should sublease your Boston place," Dottie said.

I slotted in a disk, as I'd learned to do, and popped some keys.

"That's cute," Dottie said.

"Well, it works. Would you like it? You may have it," I said.

"The inn has its own, for reservations and all. I keep it stored away off season," Dottie said. She puttered off to get the mail.

"I could never work on this one," I said.

I retrieved, read, and deleted the long poem I had written on the road. There was nothing in there of Raymond or Mississippi or Raf or the storm that had seemed to follow me; nothing of driving or dreaming or hoping or falling down or phone calls or missing anybody.

Around six, Mario came with a double armload of fresh flowers for Dottie. He was dressed in a black suit, starched shirt, and a massive scarf looped around his throat three times.

"Isn't he striking?" Dottie said. She wore a fake fur over her winter-white sweater dress.

"He's gorgeous," I said.

"I'm think of poor Zerlina in *Don Giovanni*," Mario said. " 'You may yet be making fun of me.' "

"Never. We wouldn't," Dottie said.

"So then, we go," he said.

"Get her home by twelve," I said. "And don't try to hand me the flat tire on the freeway routine."

"She should no try to be funny, because it's not," Mario said.

"Listen to your father, Paige," said Dottie.

I met Raf in Cambridge. We walked and did some book-store browsing, walked on cobblestone streets of brick townhouses and row houses, many with wreaths on their doors; past rambling mansions and their snowy expanses of lawn; stands of pine, willow, and birch trees.

In Wordsmith, I watched as Raf wandered an aisle. He shambled spent, like a person who had been doing heavy lifting. He stretched, rubbed his arms in their coat sleeves. In his athletic periods I often saw him working kinks from his joints this way. I wondered if Raf understood what his last event had been.

"What're we doin' after this?" he asked me. He flumped an armload of paperbacks onto the cash-register desk.

I couldn't decide what was next. The speakers in the place were sounding Beethoven, the *Archduke Trio*. I got lost listening, and thinking of an old Godard movie: of a man and woman in bed, in smoky sunlight, a couple with something enormous to lose.

Raf said, "You want to go for coffee or just quit? You seem kind of runover."

"I want to go for a three-week drive."

"I always want to do that," Raf said.

"You pilot if you want," I told him.

"I want," he said.

He swung the smoke-colored car away from the Cam-bridge garage. He drove with a kind of weary aggression —kicking at the clutch, slugging the gear stick.

I talked about the streets in Cameroon, how some days they were full of sand, almost impassable from sand. People would sweep but more sand would come, covering and ruining everything.

We got on and off the Mass. Turnpike.

Raf plunged in the clutch pedal, let the car slow and roll onto the shoulder of the road. He braked. The headlights showed over lapping layers of mist slicking the twisting lane ahead. The windshield wipers slithered left and right. Their motor hummed.

He reached under his seat and tugged out a road atlas.

"Don't worry," he said, reading a map. He said "worry" with a tone of puzzlement for anyone who might.

I studied him. Below his black hair the fine bones of his skull were modeled by the white cabin light. His good eye was a pool of shadow. I thought: generic man, perfect man. I thought how even when Raf was dead-still, he had an intensity out of which someone could interpret a world.

A NOTE ON THE TYPE

The text of this book was set in Sabon, a typeface
designed by Jan Tschichold (1902–1974), the well-known
German typographer. Because it was designed in Frankfurt,
Sabon was named for the famous Frankfurt type founder
Jacques Sabon, who died in 1580 while manager
of the Egenolff foundry.
Based loosely on the original designs of
Claude Garamond (c. 1480–1561), Sabon is unique
in that it was explicitly designed for hot-metal
composition on both the Monotype and Linotype
machines as well as for film composition.

Composed by Crane Typesetting Service, Inc.
West Barnstable, Massachusetts
Printed and bound by Arcata Graphics,
Martinsburg, West Virginia
Designed by Mia Vander Els

Mary Robison was born in Washington, D.C., in 1949.
Besides *Subtraction* and her 1981 novel, *Oh!*, she has written
short stories and screenplays. For the past twelve years, she has taught
at various universities, including the University of Houston and
Harvard. She lives in Texas.